12⁹⁵

Tears
of the
Giraffe

Alexander McCall Smith

Tears
of the
Giraffe

africa
africa africa
africa africa africa
africa africa
africa

POLYGON

EDINBURGH

First published by
Polygon
22 George Square
Edinburgh
EH8 9LF

Printed and bound in Great Britain by
Bell & Bain Ltd, Glasgow.

A CIP record is available for this title.

ISBN 0 7486 6273 1

The Publisher acknowledges subsidy from

towards the publication of this volume.

*This book is for
Richard Latcham*

CHAPTER ONE

Mr J.L.B. Matekoni's House

Mr J.L.B. Matekoni, proprietor of Tlokweng Road Speedy Motors, found it difficult to believe that Mma Ramotswe, the accomplished founder of the No. 1 Ladies' Detective Agency, had agreed to marry him. It was at the second time of asking; the first posing of the question, which had required immense courage on his part, had brought forth a refusal – gentle, and regretful – but a refusal nonetheless. After that, he had assumed that Mma Ramotswe would never remarry; that her brief and disastrous marriage to Note Mokoti, trumpeter and jazz aficionado, had persuaded her that marriage was nothing but a recipe for sorrow and suffering. After all, she was an independent-minded woman, with a business to run, and a comfortable house of her own in Zebra Drive. Why, he wondered, should a woman like that take on a man, when a man could prove to be difficult to manage once vows were exchanged and he had settled himself in her house? No, if he were in Mma Ramotswe's shoes, then he might well decline an offer of marriage, even from somebody as eminently reasonable and respectable as himself.

But then, on that noumenal evening, sitting with him on her verandah after he had spent the afternoon fixing her tiny white van, she had said yes. And she had given this answer in such a simple, unambiguously *kind* way, that he had been confirmed in his belief that she was one of the very best women in Botswana. That evening, when he returned home to his house near the old Defence Force Club, he had reflected on the enormity of his good fortune. Here he was, in his mid-forties, a man who had until that point been unable to find a suitable wife, now blessed with the hand of the one woman whom he admired more than any other. Such remarkable good fortune was almost inconceivable, and he wondered whether he would suddenly wake up from the delicious dream into which he seemed to have wandered.

Yet it was true. The next morning, when he turned on his bedside radio to hear the familiar sound of cattle bells with which Radio Botswana prefaced its morning broadcast, he realised that it had indeed happened and that unless she had changed her mind overnight, he was a man engaged to be married.

He looked at his watch. It was six o'clock, and the first light of the day was on the thorn tree outside his bedroom window. Smoke from morning fires, the fine wood smoke that sharpened the appetite, would soon be in the air, and he would hear the sound of people on the paths that criss-crossed the bush near his house; shouts of children on their way to school; men going sleepy-eyed to their work in the town; women calling out to one another; Africa waking up and starting the day. People arose early, but it would be best to wait an hour or so before he telephoned Mma Ramotswe, which would give her time to get up and make her morning cup of bush tea. Once she had done that, he knew that she liked to sit outside for half an hour or so and watch the birds on her patch of grass. There were hoopoes, with their black and white stripes, pecking at insects like little mechanical toys, and the strutting ring-neck doves, engaged in their constant wooing. Mma Ramotswe liked birds, and perhaps, if she were interested, he could build her an aviary. They could breed doves, maybe, or even, as some people did, something bigger, such as buzzards, though what they would do with buzzards once they had bred them was not clear. They ate snakes, of course, and that would be useful, but a dog was just as good a means of keeping snakes out of the yard.

When he was a boy out at Molepolole, Mr J.L.B. Matekoni had owned a dog which had established itself as a legendary snake-catcher. It was a thin brown animal, with one or two white patches, and a broken tail. He had found it, abandoned and half-starved, at the edge of the village, and had taken it home to live with him at his grandmother's house. She had been unwilling to waste food on an animal that had no apparent function, but he had won her round and the dog had stayed. Within a few weeks it had proved its usefulness, killing three snakes in the yard and one in a neighbour's melon patch. From then on, its reputation was assured, and if anybody was having trouble with snakes they would ask Mr J.L.B. Matekoni to bring his dog round to deal with the problem.

The dog was preternaturally quick. Snakes, when they saw it coming, seemed to know that they were in mortal danger. The dog, hair bristling and eyes bright with excitement, would move towards the snake with a curious gait, as if it were standing on the tips of its claws. Then, when it was within a few feet of its quarry, it would utter a low growl, which the snake would sense as a vibration in the ground. Momentarily confused, the snake would usually begin to slide away, and it at this point that the dog would launch itself forward and nip the snake neatly behind the head. This broke its back, and the struggle was over.

Mr J.L.B. Matekoni knew that such dogs never reached old age. If they survived to the age of seven or eight, their reactions begin to slow and the odds shifted slowly in favour of the snake. Mr J.L.B. Matekoni's dog eventually fell victim to a banded cobra, and died within minutes of the bite. There was no dog who could replace him, but now ... Well, this was just another possibility that opened up. They could buy a dog and choose its name together. Indeed, he would suggest that she choose both the dog and the name, as he was keen that Mma Ramotswe should not feel that he was trying to take all the decisions. In fact, he would be happy to take as few decisions as possible. She was a very competent woman, and he had complete confidence in her ability to run their life together, as long as she did not try to involve him in her detective business. That was simply not what he had in mind. She was the detective; he was the mechanic. That was how matters should remain.

He telephoned shortly before seven. Mma Ramotswe seemed pleased to hear from him and asked him, as was polite in the Setswana language, whether he had slept well.

"I slept very well," said Mr J.L.B. Matekoni. "I dreamed all the night about that clever and beautiful woman who has agreed to marry me."

He paused. If she was going to announce a change of mind, then this was the time that she might be expected to do it.

Mma Ramotswe laughed. "I never remember what I dream," she said. "But if I did, then I am sure that I would remember dreaming about that first-class mechanic who is going to be my husband one day."

Mr J.L.B. Matekoni smiled with relief. She had not thought better of it, and they were still engaged.

"Today we must go to the President Hotel for lunch," he said. "We shall have to celebrate this important matter."

Mma Ramotswe agreed. She would be ready at twelve o'clock and afterwards, if it was convenient, perhaps he would allow her to visit his house to see what it was like. There would be two houses now, and they would have to choose one. Her house on Zebra Drive had many good qualities, but it was rather close to the centre of town and there was a case for being further away. His house, near the old air field, had a larger yard and was undoubtedly quieter, but was not far from the prison and was there not an overgrown grave-yard nearby? That was a major factor; if she were alone in the house at night for any reason, it would not do to be too close to a graveyard. Not that Mma Ramotswe was supersti-tious; her theology was conventional and had little room for unquiet spirits and the like, and yet, and yet ...

In Mma Ramotswe's view there was God, *Modimo*, who lived in the sky, more or less directly above Africa. God was extremely understanding, particularly of people like herself, but to break his rules, as so many people did with complete disregard, was to invite retribution. When they died, good people, such as Mma Ramotswe's father, Obed Ramotswe, were undoubtedly welcomed by God. The fate of the others was unclear, but they were sent to some terrible place – perhaps a bit like Nigeria, she thought – and when they ac-knowledged their wrongdoing they would be forgiven.

God had been kind to her, thought Mma Ramotswe. He had given her a happy childhood, even if her mother had been taken from her when she was a baby. She had been looked after by her father and her kind cousin and they had taught her what it was to give love – love which she had in turn given, over those few precious days, to her tiny baby. When the child's battle for life had ended, she had briefly wondered why God had done this to her, but in time she had understood. Now his kindness to her was manifest again, this time in the appearance of Mr J.L.B. Matekoni, a good kind, man. God had sent her a husband.

After their celebration lunch in the President Hotel – a lunch at which Mr J.L.B. Matekoni ate two large steaks and Mma Ramotswe, who had a sweet tooth, dipped into rather more ice cream than she had originally intended – they drove off in Mr J.L.B. Matekoni's pickup truck to inspect his house.

"It is not a very tidy house," said Mr J.L.B.Matekoni,

anxiously. "I try to keep it tidy, but that is a difficult thing for a man. There is a maid who comes in, but she makes it worse, I think. She is a very untidy woman."

"We can keep the woman who works for me," said Mma Ramotswe. "She is very good at everything. Ironing. Cleaning. Polishing. She is one of the best people in Botswana for all these tasks. We can find some other work for your person."

"And there are some rooms in his house that have got motor parts in them," added Mr J.L.B. Matekoni hurriedly. "Sometimes I have not had enough room at the garage and have had to store them in the house – interesting engines that I might need some day."

Mma Ramotswe said nothing. She now knew why Mr J.L.B. Matekoni had never invited her to the house before. His office at Tlokweng Road Speedy Motors was bad enough, with all that grease and those calendars that the parts suppliers sent him. They were ridiculous calendars, in her view, with all those far-too-thin ladies sitting on tyres and leaning against cars. Those ladies were useless for everything. They would not be good for having children, and not one of them looked as if she had her school certificate, or even her standard six. They were useless, good-time girls, who only made men all hot and bothered, and that was no good to anybody. If only men knew what fools of them these bad girls made; but they did not know it and it was hopeless trying to point it out to them.

They arrived at the entrance to his driveway and Mma Ramotswe sat in the car while Mr J.L.B. Matekoni pushed open the silver-painted gate. She noted that the dustbin had been pushed open by dogs and that scraps of paper and other rubbish were lying about. If she were to move here – *if* – that would soon be stopped. In traditional Botswana society, keeping the yard in good order was a woman's responsibility, and she would certainly not wish to be associated with a yard like this.

They parked in front of the stoep, under a rough car shelter that Mr J.L.B. Matekoni had fashioned out of shade-netting. It was a large house by modern standards, built in a day when builders had no reason to worry about space. There was the whole of Africa in those days, most of it unused, and nobody bothered to save space. Now it was different, and people had begun to worry about cities and how they gobbled up the bush surrounding them. This house, a low, rather gloomy bungalow under a corrugated-tin roof, had been built for a colonial official in Protectorate days. The outer walls were plastered and whitewashed, and the floors were polished red cement, laid out in large squares. Such floors always seemed cool on the feet in the hot months, although for real comfort it was hard to better the beaten mud or cattle dung of traditional floors.

Mma Ramotswe looked about her. They were in the living room, into which the front door gave immediate entrance. There was a heavy suite of furniture – expensive in its day – but now looking distinctly down-at-heel. The chairs, which had wide wooden arms, were upholstered in red, and there was a table of black hardwood on which an empty glass and an ashtray stood. On the walls there was picture of a mountain, painted on dark velvet, a wooden kudu-head, and a small picture of Nelson Mandela. The whole effect was perfectly pleasing, thought Mma Ramotswe, although it certainly had that forlorn look so characteristic of an unmarried man's room.

"This is a very fine room," observed Mma Ramotswe.

Mr J.L.B. Matekoni beamed with pleasure. "I try to keep this room tidy," he said. "It is important to have a special room for important visitors."

"Do you have any important visitors?" asked Mma

Ramotswe.

Mr J.L.B. Matekoni frowned. "There have been none so far," he said. "But it is always possible."

"Yes," agreed Mma Ramotswe. "One never knows."

She looked over her shoulder, towards a door that led into the rest of the house.

"The other rooms are that way?" she asked politely.

Mr J.L.B. Matekoni nodded. "That is the not-so-tidy part of the house," he said. "Perhaps we should look at it some other time."

Mma Ramotswe shook her head and Mr J.L.B. Matekoni realised that there was no escape. This was part and parcel of marriage, he assumed; there could be no secrets – everything had to be laid bare.

"This way," he said tentatively, opening the door. "Really, I must get a better maid. She is not doing her job at all well."

Mma Ramotswe followed him down the corridor. The first door that they reached was half open, and she stopped at the doorway and peered in. The room, which had obviously once been a bedroom, had its floors covered with newspapers, laid out as if they were a carpet. In the middle of the floor sat an engine, its cylinders exposed, while around it on the floor there were littered the parts that had been taken from the engine.

"That is a very special engine," said Mr J.L.B. Matekoni, looking at her anxiously. "There is no other engine like it in Botswana. One day I shall finish fixing it."

They moved on. The next room was a bathroom, which was clean enough, thought Mma Ramotswe, even if rather stark and neglected. On the edge of the bath, balanced on an old white face-cloth, was a large bar of carbolic soap. Apart from that, there was nothing.

"Carbolic soap is very healthy soap," said Mr J.L.B. Matekoni. "I have always used it."

Mma Ramotswe nodded. She favoured palm-oil soap, which was good for the complexion, but she understood that men liked something more bracing. It was a bleak bathroom, she thought, but at least it was clean.

Of the remaining rooms, only one was habitable, the dining room, which had a table in the middle and a solitary chair. Its floor, however, was dirty, with piles of dust under the furniture and in each corner. Whoever was meant to be cleaning this room had clearly not swept it for months. What did she do, this maid? Did she stand at the gate and talk to her friends, as they tended to do if not watched closely? It was clear to Mma Ramotswe that the maid was taking gross advantage of Mr J.L.B. Matekoni and relying on his good nature to keep her job.

The other rooms, although they contained beds, were cluttered with boxes stuffed with spark plugs, windscreen-wiper blades, and other curious mechanical pieces. And as for the kitchen, this, although clean, was again virtually bare, containing only two pots, several white enamelled plates, and a small cutlery tray.

"This maid is meant to cook for me," said Mr J.L.B. Matekoni. "She makes a meal each day, but it is always the same. All that I have to eat is maizemeal and stew. Sometimes she cooks me pumpkin, but not very often. And yet she always seems to need lots of money for kitchen supplies."

"She is a very lazy woman," said Mma Ramotswe. "She should be ashamed of herself. If all women in Botswana were like that, our men would have died out a long time ago."

Mr J.L.B. Matekoni smiled. His maid had held him in thrall for years, and he had never had the courage to stand up to her. But now perhaps she had met her match in Mma Ramotswe, and she would soon be looking for somebody else to neglect.

[9]

"Where is this woman?" asked Mma Ramotswe. "I would like to talk to her."

Mr J.L.B. Matekoni looked at his watch. "She should be here soon," he said. "She comes here every afternoon at about this time."

They were sitting in the living room when the maid arrived, announcing her presence with the slamming of the kitchen door.

"That is her," said Mr J.L.B. Matekoni. "She always slams doors. She has never closed a door quietly in all the years she has worked here. It's always slam, slam."

"Let's go through and see her," said Mma Ramotswe. "I'm interested to meet this lady who has been looking after you so well."

Mr J.L.B. Matekoni led the way into the kitchen. In front of the sink, where she was filling a kettle with water, stood a large woman in her mid-thirties. She was markedly taller than both Mr J.L.B. Matekoni and Mma Ramotswe, and, although rather thinner than Mma Ramotswe, she looked considerably stronger, with bulging biceps and well-set legs. She was wearing a large, battered red hat on her head and a blue house coat over her dress. Her shoes were made of a curious, shiny leather, rather like the patent leather used to make dancing pumps.

Mr J.L.B. Matekoni cleared his throat, to reveal their presence, and the maid turned round slowly.

"I am busy ..." she started to say, but stopped, seeing Mma Ramotswe.

Mr J.L.B. Matekoni greeted her politely, in the traditional way. Then he introduced his guest. "This is Mma Ramotswe," he said.

The maid looked at Mma Ramotswe and nodded curtly.

"I am glad that I have had the chance to meet you, Mma,"

said Mma Ramotswe. "I have heard about you from Mr J.L.B. Matekoni."

The maid glanced at her employer. "Oh, you have heard of me," she said. "I am glad that he speaks of me. I would not like to think that nobody speaks of me."

"No," said Mma Ramotswe. "It is better to be spoken of than not to be spoken of. Except sometimes, that is."

The maid frowned. The kettle was now full and she took it from under the tap.

"I am very busy," she said dismissively. "There is much to do in this house."

"Yes," said Mma Ramotswe. 'There is certainly a great deal to do. A dirty house like this needs a lot of work doing in it."

The large maid stiffened. "Why do you say this house is dirty?" she said. "Who are you to say that this house is dirty?"

"She ..." began Mr J.L.B. Matekoni, but he was silenced by a glare from the maid and he stopped.

"I say that because I have seen it," said Mma Ramotswe. "I have seen all the dust in the dining room and all the rubbish in the garden. Mr J.L.B. Matekoni here is only a man. He cannot be expected to keep his own house clean."

The maid's eyes had opened wide and were staring at Mma Ramotswe with ill-disguised venom. Her nostrils were flared with anger, and her lips were pushed out in what seemed to be an aggressive pout.

"I have worked for this man for many years," she hissed. "Every day I have worked, worked, worked. I have made him good food and polished the floor. I have looked after him very well."

"I don't think so, Mma," said Mma Ramotswe calmly. "If you have been feeding him so well, then why is he thin? A man who is well looked-after becomes fatter. They are just like cattle. That is well known."

[11]

The maid shifted her gaze from Mma Ramotswe to her employer. "Who is this woman?" she demanded. "Why is she coming into my kitchen and saying things like this? Please ask her to go back to the bar you found her in."

Mr J.L.B. Matekoni swallowed hard. "I have asked her to marry me," he blurted out. "She is going to be my wife."

At this, the maid seemed to crumple. "Aiee!" she cried. "Aiee! You cannot marry her! She will kill you! That is the worst thing you can do."

Mr J.L.B. Matekoni moved forward and placed a comforting hand on the maid's shoulder.

"Do not worry, Florence," he said. "She is a good woman, and I shall make sure that you will get another job. I have a cousin who has that hotel near the bus station. He needs maids and if I ask him to give you a job he will do so."

This did not pacify the maid. "I do not want to work in a hotel, where everyone is treated like a slave," she said. "I am not a do-this, do-that maid. I am a high-class maid, suitable for private houses. Oh! Oh! I am finished now. You are finished too if you marry this fat woman. She will break your bed. You will surely die very quickly. This is the end for you."

Mr J.L.B. Matekoni glanced at Mma Ramotswe, signalling that they should leave the kitchen. It would be better, he thought, if the maid could recover in private. He had not imagined that the news would be well received, but he had certainly not envisaged her uttering such embarrassing and disturbing prophecies. The sooner he spoke to the cousin and arranged the transfer to the other job, the better.

They went back to the sitting room, closing the door firmly behind them.

"Your maid is a difficult woman," said Mma Ramotswe.

"She is not easy," said Mr J.L.B. Matekoni. "But I think that we have no choice. She must go to that other job."

Mma Ramotswe nodded. He was right. The maid would

have to go, but so would they. They could not live in this house, she thought, even if it had a bigger yard. They would have to put in a tenant and move to Zebra Drive. Her own maid was infinitely better and would look after both of them extremely well. In no time at all, Mr J.L.B. Matekoni would begin to put on weight, and look more like the prosperous garage owner he was. She glanced about the room. Was there anything at all that they would need to move from this house to hers? The answer, she thought, was probably no. All that Mr J.L.B. Matekoni needed to bring was a suitcase containing his clothes and his bar of carbolic soap. That was all.

CHAPTER TWO

A Client Arrives

IT WOULD HAVE to be handled tactfully. Mma Ramotswe knew that Mr J.L.B. Matekoni would be happy to live in Zebra Drive – she was sure of that – but men had their pride and she would have to be careful about how she conveyed the decision. She could hardly say: "Your house is a terrible mess; there are engines and car parts everywhere." Nor could she say: "I would not like to live that close to an old graveyard." Rather, she would approach it by saying: "It's a wonderful house, with lots of room. I don't mind old engines at all, but I am sure you will agree that Zebra Drive is very convenient for the centre of town." That would be the way to do it.

She had already worked out how the arrival of Mr J.L.B. Matekoni could be catered for in her house in Zebra Drive. Her house was not quite as large as his, but they would have more than enough room. There were three bedrooms. They would occupy the biggest of these, which was also the quietest, being at the back. She currently used the other two rooms for storage and for sewing, but she could clear out the storage room and put everything it contained in the garage. That would make a room for Mr J.L.B. Matekoni's private use. Whether he wished to use it to store car parts or old engines would be up to him, but a very strong hint would be given that engines should stay outside.

The living room could probably stay more or less unchanged. Her own chairs were infinitely preferable to the furniture she had seen in his sitting room, although he may well wish to bring the velvet picture of the mountain and one or two of his ornaments. These would complement her own possessions, which included the photograph of her father, her daddy, as she called him, Obed Ramotswe, in his favourite shiny suit, the photograph before which she stopped so often and thought of his life and all that it meant to her. She was sure that he would have approved of Mr J.L.B. Matekoni. He had warned her against Note Mokoti, although he had not tried to stop the marriage, as some parents might have done. She had been aware of his feelings but had been too young, and too infatuated with the plausible trumpet player, to take account of what her father thought. And, when the marriage had ended so disastrously, he had not spoken of his presentment that this was exactly what would happen, but had been concerned only about her safety and her happiness – which is how he had always been. She was lucky to have had such a father, she thought; today there were so many people without a father, people who were being brought up by their mothers or their grandmothers and who in many cases did not even know who their father was. They seemed happy enough, it seemed, but there must always be a great gap in their lives. Perhaps if you don't know there's a gap, you don't worry about it. If you were a millipede, a *tshongololo*, crawling along the ground would you look at the birds and worry about not having wings? Probably not.

Mma Ramotswe was given to philosophical speculation, but only up to a point. Such questions were undoubtedly challenging, but they tended to lead to further questions which simply could not be answered. And at that point one ended up, as often as not, having to accept that things are as they are simply because that is the way they are. So everybody knew, for instance, that it was wrong for a man to be too close to a place where a woman is giving birth. That was something which was so obvious that it hardly needed to be stated. But then there were these remarkable ideas in other countries that suggested that men should actually attend the birth of their children. When Mma Ramotswe read about that in a magazine, her breath was taken away. But then she had asked herself why a father should not see his child being born, so that he could welcome it into the world and share the joy of the occasion, and she had found it difficult to find a reason. That is not to say it was not wrong – there was no question that it was profoundly wrong for a man to be there – but how could one justify the prohibition? Ultimately the answer must be that it was wrong because the old Botswana morality said that it was wrong, and the old Botswana morality, as everybody knew, was so plainly right. It just *felt* right.

Nowadays, of course, there were plenty of people who appeared to be turning away from that morality. She saw it in the behaviour of schoolchildren, who strutted about and pushed their way around with scant respect for older people. When she was at school, children respected adults and lowered their eyes when they spoke to them, but now children looked straight at you and answered back. She had recently told a young boy – barely thirteen, she thought – to pick up an empty can that he had tossed on the ground in the mall the other day. He had looked at her in amazement, and had then laughed and told her that she could pick it up if she liked as he had no intention of doing so. She had been so astonished by his cheek that she had been unable to think of a suitable riposte, and he had sauntered away, leaving her speechless. When she was young, a woman would have picked up a boy like that and spanked him on the spot. But today you couldn't spank other people's children in the street; if you tried to do so there would be an enormous fuss. She was a modern lady, of course, and did not approve of spanking, but sometimes one had to wonder. Would that boy have dropped the can in the first place if knew that somebody might spank him? Probably not.

Thoughts about marriage, and moving house, and spanking boys, were all very well but everyday life still required to be attended to, and for Mma Ramotswe, this meant that she had to open up the No. 1 Ladies' Detective Agency on Monday morning, as she did on every working morning, even if there was very little possibility of anybody coming in with an enquiry or telephoning. Mma Ramotswe felt that it was important to keep one's word, and the sign outside the agency announced that the opening hours were from nine in the morning until five in the afternoon, every day. In fact, no client had ever consulted her until well into the morning, and usually clients came in the late afternoon. Why this should be, she had no idea, although she sometimes reflected that it took people some time to build up the courage to cross her threshold and admit to whatever it was that was troubling them.

So Mma Ramotswe sat with her secretary, Mma Makutsi, and drank the large mug of bush tea which Mma Makutsi brewed for them both at the beginning of each day. She did not really need a secretary, but a business which wished to be taken seriously required somebody to answer the telephone or to take calls if she was out. Mma Makutsi was a highly-skilled typist – she had scored 97 per cent in her secretarial examinations – and was probably wasted on a small business such as this, but she was good company, and loyal, and, most important of all, had a gift for discretion.

"We must not talk about what we see in this business," Mma Ramotswe had stressed when she engaged her, and Mma Makutsi had nodded solemnly. Mma Ramotswe did not expect her to understand confidentiality – people in Botswana liked to talk about what was happening – and she was surprised when she found out that Mma Makutsi understood very well what the obligation of confidentiality entailed. Indeed, Mma Ramotswe had discovered that her secretary even refused to tell people where she worked, referring only to an office "somewhere over near Kgale Hill". This was somewhat unnecessary, but at least it was an indication that the clients' confidences would be safe with her.

Early morning tea with Mma Makutsi was a comforting ritual, but it was also useful from the professional point of view. Mma Makutsi was extremely observant, and she also listened attentively for any little snippet of gossip that could be useful. It was from her, for instance, that Mma Ramotswe had heard that a medium-ranking official in the planning department was proposing to marry the sister of the woman who owned Ready Now Dry Cleaners. This information may have seemed mundane, but when Mma Ramotswe had been engaged by a supermarket owner to discover why he was being denied a licence to build a dry-cleaning agency next to his supermarket, it was useful to be able to point out that the person making the decision may have an interest in another, rival dry-cleaning establishment. That information alone stopped the nonsense; all that Mma Ramotswe had needed to do was to point out to the official that there were people in Gaborone who were saying – surely without any justification – that he might allow his business connections to influence his judgement. Of course, when somebody had mentioned this to her, she had disputed the rumour vehemently, and had argued that there could be no possible connection between his dry-cleaning associations and the difficulty which anybody else might be having over getting a licence to open up such a business. The very thought was outrageous, she had said.

On that Monday, Mma Makutsi had nothing of significance to report. She had enjoyed a quiet weekend with her sister, who was a nurse at the Princess Marina Hospital. They had bought some material and had started to make a dress for the sister's daughter. On Sunday they had gone to church and a woman had fainted during one of the hymns. Her sister had helped to revive her and they had made her some tea in the hall at the side of the church. The woman was too fat, she said, and the heat had been too much for her, but she had recovered quickly and had drunk four cups of tea. She was a woman from the north, she said, and she twelve children up in Francistown.

"That is too much," said Mma Ramotswe. "In these modern days, it is not a good thing to have twelve children. The Government should tell people to stop after six. Six is enough, or maybe seven or eight if you can afford to feed that many."

Mma Makutsi agreed. She had four brothers and two sisters and she thought that this had prevented her parents from paying adequate attention to the education of each of them.

"It was a miracle that I got 97 per cent," she said.

'If there had only been three children, then you would have got over one hundred per cent," observed Mma Ramotswe.

"Impossible," said Mma Makutsi. "Nobody has ever got over one hundred per cent in the history of the Botswana Secretarial College. It's just not possible."

They were not busy that morning. Mma Makutsi cleaned her typewriter and polished her desk, while Mma Ramotswe read a magazine and wrote a letter to her cousin in Lobatse. The hours passed slowly, and by twelve o'clock Mma Ramotswe was prepared to shut the agency for lunch. But just as she was about to suggest that to Mma Makutsi, her secretary slammed a drawer shut, inserted a piece of paper into her typewriter and began to type energetically. This signalled the arrival of a client.

A large car, covered in the ubiquitous thin layer of dust that settled on everything in the dry season, had drawn up and a thin, white woman, wearing a khaki blouse and khaki trousers had stepped out of the passenger seat. She glanced up briefly at the sign on the front of the building, took off her sunglasses, and knocked on the half-open door.

Mma Makutsi admitted her to the office, while Mma Ramotswe rose from her chair to welcome her.

"I'm sorry to come without an appointment," said the woman. "I hope that I might find you in."

"You don't need an appointment," said Mma Ramotswe warmly, reaching out to shake her hand. "You are always welcome."

The woman took her hand, correctly, Mma Ramotswe noticed, in the proper Botswana way, placing her left hand on her right forearm as a mark of respect. Most white people shook hands very rudely, snatching just one hand and leaving their other hand free to perform all sorts of mischief. This woman had at least learned something about how to behave.

She invited the caller to sit down in the chair which they kept for clients, while Mma Makutsi busied herself with the kettle.

"I'm Mrs Andrea Curtin," said the visitor. "I heard from somebody in my embassy that you were a detective and you might be able to help me."

Mma Ramotswe raised an eyebrow. "Embassy?"

"The American Embassy," said Mrs Curtin. "I asked them to give me the name of a detective agency."

Mma Ramotswe smiled. "I am glad that they recommended me," she said. "But what do you need?"

The woman had folded her hands on her lap and now she looked down at them. The skin of her hands was mottled, Mma Ramotswe noticed, in the way that white peoples' hands were if they were exposed to too much sun. Perhaps she was an American who had lived for many years in Africa; there were many of these people. They grew to love Africa and they stayed, sometimes until they died. Mma Ramotswe could understand why they did this. She could not imagine why anybody would want to live anywhere else. How did people survive in cold, northern climates, with all that snow and rain and darkness?

"I could say that I am looking for somebody," said Mrs Curtin, raising her eyes to meet Mma Ramotswe's gaze. "But then that would suggest that there is somebody to look for. I don't think that there is. So I suppose I should say that I'm trying to find out what happened to somebody, quite a long time ago. I don't expect that that person is alive. In fact, I am certain that he is not. But I want to find out what happened."

Mma Ramotswe nodded. "Sometimes it is important to know," she said. "And I am sorry, Mma, if you have lost somebody."

Mr Curtin smiled. "You're very kind. Yes, I lost somebody."

"When was this?" asked Mma Ramotswe.

"Ten years ago," said Mrs Curtin. "Ten years ago I lost my son."

For a few moments there was a silence. Mma Ramotswe glanced over to where Mma Makutsi was standing near the sink and noticed that her secretary was watching Mrs Curtin attentively. When she caught her employer's gaze, Mma Makutsi looked guilty and returned to her task of filling the teapot.

Mma Ramotswe broke the silence. "I am very sorry. I know what it is like to lose a child."

"Do you, Mma?"

She was not sure whether the question had an edge to it, as if it were a challenge, but she answered gently. "I lost my baby. He did not live."

Mrs Curtin lowered her gaze. "Then you know," she said.

Mma Makutsi had now prepared the bush tea and she

[21]

brought over a chipped enamel tray on which two mugs were standing. Mrs Curtin took hers gratefully, and began to sip on the hot, red liquid.

"I should tell you something about myself," said Mrs Curtin. "Then you will know why I am here and why I would like you to help me. If you can help me I shall be very pleased, but if not, I shall understand."

"I will tell you," said Mma Ramotswe. "I cannot help everybody. I will not waste our time or your money. I shall tell you whether I can help."

Mrs Curtin put down her mug and wiped her hand against the side of her khaki trousers.

"Then let me tell you," she said, "why an American woman is sitting in your office in Botswana. Then, at the end of what I have to say, you can say either yes or no. It will be that simple. Either yes or no."

CHAPTER THREE

The Boy with an African Heart

I CAME TO Africa twelve years ago. I was forty-three and Africa meant nothing to me. I suppose I had the usual ideas about it – a hotchpotch of images of big game and savannah and Kilimanjaro rising out of the cloud. I also thought of famines and civil wars and potbellied, half-naked children staring at the camera, sunk in hopelessness. I know that all that is just one side of it – and not the most important side either – but it was what was in my mind.

My husband was an economist. We met in college and married shortly after we graduated; we were very young, but our marriage lasted. He took a job in Washington and ended up in the World Bank. He became quite senior there and could have spent his entire career in Washington, going up the ladder there. But he became restless, and one day he announced that there was a posting available to spend two years here in Botswana as a regional manager for World Bank activities in this part of Africa. It was promotion, after all, and if it was a cure for restlessness then I thought it preferable to his having an affair with another woman, which is the other way that men cure their restlessness. You know how it is, Mma, when men realize that they are no longer young. They panic, and they look for a younger woman who will reassure them that they are still men.

I couldn't have borne any of that, and so I agreed, and we came out here with our son, Michael, who was then just eighteen. He had been due to go to college that year, but we decided that he could have a year out with us before he started at Dartmouth. That's a very good college in America, Mma.

Some of our colleges are not very good at all, but that one is one of the best. We were proud that he had a place there.

Michael took to the idea of coming out here and began to read everything he could find on Africa. By the time we arrived he knew far more than either of us did. He read everything that van der Post had written – all that dreamy nonsense – and then he sought out much weightier things, books by anthropologists on the San and even the Moffat journals. I think this is how he first fell in love with Africa – through all those books, even before he had set foot on African soil.

The Bank had arranged a house in Gaborone, just behind State House, where all those embassies and high commissions are. I took to it at once. There had been good rains that year and the garden had been well tended. There was bed after bed of cannas and arum lilies; great riots of bougainvillaea; thick kikuyu-grass lawns. It was a little square of paradise behind a high white wall.

Michael was like a child who has just discovered the key to the candy cupboard. He would get up early in the morning and take Jack's truck out on to the Molepolole Road. Then he would walk about in the bush for an hour or so before he came back for breakfast. I went with him once or twice, even though I don't like getting up early, and he would rattle on about the birds we saw and the lizards we found scuttling about in the dust; he knew all the names within days. And we would watch the sun come up behind us, and feel its warmth. You know how it is, Mma, out there, on the edge of the Kalahari. It's the time of day when the sky is white and empty and there is that sharp smell in the air, and you just want to fill your lungs to bursting.

Jack was busy with his work and with all the people he had to meet – Government people, US aid people, financial people and so on. I had no interest in any of that, and so I just contented myself in running the house and reading and meeting some of the people I liked to have coffee with in the mornings. I also helped with the Methodist clinic. I drove people between the clinic and their villages, which was a good way of seeing a bit of the country apart from anything else. I came to know a lot about your people that way, Mma Ramotswe.

I think that I can say that I had never been happier in my life. We had found a country where the people treated one another well, with respect, and where there were values other than the grab, grab, grab which prevails back home. I felt humbled, in a way. Everything about my own country seemed so shoddy and superficial when held up against what I saw in Africa. People suffered here, and many of them had very little, but they had this wonderful feeling for others. When I first heard African people calling others – complete strangers – their brother or their sister, it sounded odd to my ears. But after a while I knew exactly what it meant and I started to think the same way. Then one day, somebody called me her sister for the first time, and I started to cry, and she could not understand why I should suddenly be so upset. And I said to her: *It is nothing. I am just crying. I am just crying.* I wish I could have called my friends "my sisters", but it would have sounded contrived and I could not do it. But that is how I felt. I was learning lessons. I had come to Africa and I was learning lessons.

Michael started to study Setswana and he made good progress. There was a man called Mr Nogana who came to the house to give him lessons four days a week. He was a man in his late sixties, a retired school teacher, and a very dignified man. He wore small, round glasses, and one of the lens was broken. I offered to buy him a replacement because I did not think that he had much money, but he shook his head and told me that he could see quite well and, thank you, it would not be necessary. They would sit on the verandah and Mr Nogana would go over Setswana grammar with him and give him the words for everything they saw: the plants in the garden, the clouds in the sky, the birds.

"Your son is learning quickly," he said to me. "He has got an African heart within him. I am just teaching that heart to speak."

Michael made his own friends. There were quite a few other Americans in Gaborone, some of whom were of a similar age to him, but he did not show much interest in these people, or in some of the other young expatriates who were there with diplomatic parents. He liked the company of local people, or of people who knew something about Africa. He spent a lot of time with a young South African exile and with a man who had been a medical volunteer in Mozambique. They were serious people, and I liked them too.

After a few months, he began to spend more and more time with a group of people who lived in an old farm house out beyond Molepolole. There was a girl there, an Afrikaner – she had come from Johannesburg a few years previously after getting into some sort of political trouble over the border. Then there was a German from Namibia, a lanky, bearded man who had ideas about agricultural improvement, and several local people from Mochudi who had worked in the Brigade movement there. I suppose that you might call it a commune of sorts, but then that would give the wrong idea. I think of communes as being the sort of place where hippies congregate and smoke *dagga*. This was not like that at all. They were all very serious, and what they really wanted to do was to grow vegetables in very dry soil.

The idea had come from Burkhardt, the German. He thought that agriculture in dry lands like Botswana and Namibia could be transformed by growing crops under shade-netting and irrigating them with droplets of water on strings. You will have seen how it works, Mma Ramotswe: the string comes down from a thin hosepipe and a droplet of water runs down the string and into the soil at the base of the plant. It really does work. I've seen it done.

Burkhardt wanted to set up a cooperative out there, based on that old farm house. He had managed to raise some money from somewhere or other and they had cleared a bit of bush and sunk a borehole. They had managed to persuade quite a number of local people to join the cooperative, and they were already producing a good crop of squash and cucumbers when I first went out there with Michael. They sold these to the hotels in Gaborone and to the hospital kitchens too.

Michael began to spend more and more time with these people, and then eventually he told us that he wanted to go out there and live with them. I was a bit concerned at first – what mother wouldn't be – but we came round to the idea when we realised how much it meant to him to be doing something for Africa. So I drove him out there one Sunday afternoon and left him there. He said that he would come into town the following week and call in and see us, which he did. He seemed blissfully happy, excited even, at the prospect of living with his new friends.

We saw a lot of him. The farm was only an hour out of town and they came in virtually every day to bring produce or get supplies. One of the Batswana members had been trained as a nurse, and he had set up a clinic of sorts which dealt with minor ailments. They wormed children and put cream on fungal infections and things like that. The Government gave them a small supply of drugs, and Burkhardt got the rest from various companies that were happy to dispose of time-expired drugs which would still work perfectly well. Dr Merriweather was at the Livingstone Hospital then, and he used to call in from time to time to see that everything was in order. He told me once that the nurse was every bit as good as most doctors would be.

The time came for Michael to return to America. He had to be at Dartmouth by the third week of August, and in late July he told us that he did not intend to go. He wanted to stay in Botswana for at least another year, he said. He had contacted Dartmouth, without our knowing it, and they had agreed to defer his taking up his place for a year. I was alarmed, as you can imagine. You just have to go to college in the States, you see. If you don't, then you'll never get a job worth anything. And I had visions of Michael abandoning his education and spending the rest of his life in a commune. I suppose many parents have thought the same when their children have gone off to do something idealistic.

Jack and I discussed it for hours and he persuaded me that it would be best to go along with what Michael proposed. If we attempted to persuade him otherwise, then he could just dig in further and refuse to go at all. If we agreed to his plan, then he might be happier to leave when we did, at the end of the following year.

"It's good work that he's doing," Jack said. "Most people of his age are utterly selfish. He's not like that."

And I had to agree he was right. It seemed completely right to be doing what he was doing. Botswana was a place where people believed that work of that sort could make a difference. And remember that people had to do something to show that there was real alternative to what was happening in South Africa. Botswana was a beacon in those days.

So Michael stayed where he was and of course when the time came for us to leave he refused to accompany us. He still had work to do, he said, and he wanted to spend a few more years doing it. The farm was thriving; they had sunk several more boreholes and they were providing a living for twenty families. It was too important to give up.

I had anticipated this – I think we both had. We tried to persuade him, but it was no use. Besides, he had now taken up with the South African woman, although she was a good six or seven years older than he was. I thought that she might be the real drawing factor, and we offered to help her come back with us to the States, but he refused to entertain the notion. It was Africa, he said, that was keeping him there; if we thought that it was something as simple as a relationship with a woman then we misunderstood the situation.

We left him with a fairly substantial amount of money. I am in the fortunate position of having a fund which was set up for me by my father and it meant very little to leave him with money. I knew that there was a risk that Burkhardt would persuade him to give the money over to the farm, or use it to build a dam or whatever. But I didn't mind. It made me feel more secure to know that there were funds in Gaborone for him if he needed them.

We returned to Washington. Oddly enough, when we got back I realised exactly what it was that had prevented Michael from leaving. Everything there seemed so insincere and, well, aggressive. I missed Botswana, and not a day went past, not a day, when I would not think about it. It was like an ache. I would have given anything to be able to walk out of my house and stand under a thorn tree or look up at that great white sky. Or to hear African voices calling out to one another in the night. I even missed the October heat.

Michael wrote to us every week. His letters were full of news about the farm. I heard all about how the tomatoes were doing and about the insects which had attacked the spinach plants. It was all very vivid, and very painful to me, because I would have loved to have been there doing what he was doing, knowing that it made a difference. Nothing I could do in my life made a difference to anybody. I took on various bits of charitable work. I worked on a literacy scheme. I took library books to housebound old people. But it was nothing by comparison with what my son was doing all those miles away in Africa.

Then the letter did not arrive one week and a day or two later there was a call from the American Embassy in Botswana. My son had been reported as missing. They were looking into the matter and would let me know as soon as they had any further information.

I came over immediately and I was met at the airport by somebody I knew on the Embassy staff. He explained to me that Burkhardt had reported to the police that Michael had simply disappeared one evening. They all took their meals together, and he had been at the meal. Thereafter nobody saw him. The South African woman had no idea where he had gone and the truck which he had bought after our departure was still in its shed. There was no clue as to what had happened.

The police had questioned everybody on the farm but had come up with no further information. Nobody had seen him and nobody had any idea what might have happened. It seemed that he had been swallowed up by the night.

I went out there on the afternoon of my arrival. Burkhardt was very concerned and tried to reassure me that he would soon turn up. But he was able to offer no explanation as to why he should have taken it into his head to leave without a word to anyone. The South African woman was taciturn. She was suspicious of me, for some reason, and said very little. She, too, could think of no reason for Michael to disappear.

I stayed for four weeks. We put a notice in the newspapers and offered a reward for information as to his whereabouts. I travelled backwards and forwards to the farm, going over every possibility in my mind. I engaged a game tracker to conduct a search of the bush in the area, and he searched for two weeks before giving up. There was nothing to be found.

Eventually they decided that one of two things had happened. He had been set upon by somebody, for whatever reason, possibly in the course of a robbery, and his body had been taken away. Or he had been taken by wild animals, perhaps by a lion that had wandered in from the Kalahari. It would have been quite unusual to find a lion that close to Molepolole, but it was just possible. But if that had happened, then the game tracker would have found some clue. Yet he had come up with nothing. No spoor. No unusual animal droppings. There was nothing.

I came back a month later, and again a few months after that. Everybody was sympathetic but eventually it became apparent that they had nothing more to say to me. So I left the matter in the hands of the Embassy here and every so often they contacted the police to find out if there was any fresh news. There never was.

Six months ago Jack died. He had been ill for a while with pancreatic cancer and I had been warned that there was no hope. But after he had gone, I decided that I should try one last time to see if there was anything I could do to find out what happened to Michael. It may seem strange to you, Mma Ramotswe, that somebody should go on and on about something that happened ten years ago. But I just want to know. I just want to find out what happened to my son. I don't expect to find him. I accept that he's dead. But I would like to be able to close that chapter and say goodbye. That is all I want. Will you help me? Will you try to find out for me? You say that you lost your child. You know how I feel then. You know that, don't you? It's a sadness that never goes away. Never.

For a few moments after her visitor had finished her story,

Mma Ramotswe sat in silence. What could she do for this woman? Could she find anything out if the Botswana Police and the American Embassy had tried and failed? There was probably nothing she could do, and yet this woman needed help and if she could not obtain it from the No. 1 Ladies' Detective Agency then where would she be able to find it?

"I shall help you," she said, adding, "my sister."

CHAPTER FOUR

At the Orphan Farm

M R J.L.B. MATEKONI contemplated the view from his office at Tlokweng Road Speedy Motors. There were two windows, one of which looked directly into the workshop, where his two young apprentices were busy raising a car on a jack. They were doing it the wrong way, he noticed, in spite of his constant reminders of the dangers involved. One of them had already had an accident with the blade of an engine fan and had been lucky not to lose a finger; but they persisted with their unsafe practices. The problem, of course, was that they were barely nineteen. At this age, all young men are immortal and imagine that they will live forever. They'll find out, thought Mr J.L.B. Matekoni grimly. They'll discover that they're just like the rest of us.

He turned in his chair and looked out through the other window. The view in this direction was more pleasing: across the backyard of the garage, one could see a cluster of acacia trees sticking up out of the dry thorn scrub and, beyond that, like islands rising from a grey-green sea, the isolated hills over towards Odi. It was mid-morning and the air was still. By midday there would be a heat haze that would make the hills seem to dance and shimmer. He would go home for his lunch then as it would be too hot to work. He would sit in his kitchen, which was the coolest room of the house, eat the maizemeal and stew which his maid prepared for him, and read the *Botswana Daily News*. After that, he inevitably took a short nap before he returned to the garage and the afternoon's work.

The apprentices ate their lunch at the garage, sitting on a

couple of upturned oil drums that they had placed under one of the acacia trees. From this vantage point they watched the girls walk past and exchanged the low banter which seemed to give them such pleasure. Mr J.L.B. Matekoni had heard their conversation and had a poor opinion of it.

"You're a pretty girl! Have you got a car? I could fix your car for you. I could make you go much faster!"

This brought giggles and a quickening step from the two young typists from the Water Affairs office.

"You're too thin! You're not eating enough meat! A girl like you needs more meat so that she can have lots of children!"

"Where did you get those shoes from? Are those Mercedes Benz shoes? Fast shoes for fast girls!"

Really! thought Mr J.L.B. Matekoni. He had never behaved like that when he was their age. He had served his apprenticeship in the diesel workshops of the Botswana Bus Company and that sort of conduct would never have been tolerated. But this was the way young men behaved these days and there was nothing he could do about it. He had spoken to them about it, pointing out that the reputation of the garage depended on them just as it did on him. They had looked at him blankly, and he had realised then that they simply did not understand. They had not been taught what it was to have a reputation; the concept was completely beyond them. This realization had depressed him, and he had thought of writing to the Minister of Education about it and suggesting that the youth of Botswana be instructed in these basic moral ideas, but the letter, once composed, had sounded so pompous that he had decided not to send it. That was the difficulty, he realised. If you made any point about behaviour these days, you sounded old-fashioned and pompous. The only way to sound modern, it appeared, was to say that people could do whatever they wanted, whenever they wanted, and no matter what anybody else might think. That was the modern way of thinking.

Mr J.L.B. Matekoni transferred his gaze to his desk and to the open page of his diary. He had noted down that today was his day to go to the orphan farm; if he left immediately he could do that before lunch and be back in time to check up on his apprentices' work before the owners came to collect their cars at four o'clock. There was nothing wrong with either car; all that they required was their regular service and that was well within the range of the apprentices' ability. He had to watch them, though; they liked to tweak engines in such a way that they ran at maximum capacity, and he would often have to tune the engines down before they left the garage.

"We are not meant to be making racing cars," he reminded them. "The people who drive these cars are not speedy types like you. They are respectable citizens."

"Then why are we called Speedy Motors?" asked one of the apprentices.

Mr J.L.B. Matekoni had looked at his apprentice. There were times that he wanted to shout at him, and this perhaps was one, but he always controlled his temper.

"We are called Tlokweng Road Speedy Motors," he replied patiently, "because our *work* is speedy. Do you understand the distinction? We do not keep the customer waiting for days and days like some garages do. We turn the job round quickly, and carefully, too, as I keep having to tell you."

"Some people like speedy cars," chipped in the other apprentice. "There are some people who like to go fast."

"That may be so," said Mr J.L.B. Matekoni. "But not everyone is like that. There are some people who know that going fast is not always the best way of getting there, is it? It is better to be *late* than *the* late, is it not?"

The apprentices had stared at him uncomprehendingly, and he had sighed; again, it was the fault of the Ministry of Education and their modern ideas. These two boys would never be able to understand half of what he said. And one of these days they were going to have a bad accident.

He drove out to the orphan farm, pressing vigorously on his horn, as he always did, when he arrived at the gate. He enjoyed his visits for more than one reason. He liked to see the children, of course, and he usually brought a fistful of sweets which he would distribute when they came flocking round him. But he also liked seeing Mrs Silvia Potokwane, who was the matron in charge. She had been a friend of his mother's, and he had known her all his life. For this reason it was natural that he should take on the task of fixing any machinery which needed attending to, as well as maintaining the two trucks and the battered old minibus which served as the farm's transport. He was not paid for this, but that was not to be expected. Everybody helped the orphan farm if they could, and he would not have accepted payment had it been pressed on him.

Mma Potokwane was in her office when he arrived. She leaned out of the window and beckoned him in.

"Tea is ready, Mr J.L.B. Matekoni," she called. "There will be cake too, if you hurry."

He parked his truck under the shady boughs of a monkey-bread tree. Several children had already appeared, and skipped along beside him as he made his way to the office block.

"Have you children been good?' asked Mr J.L.B. Matekoni, reaching into his pockets.

"We have been very good children," said the oldest child. "We have been doing good things all week. We are tired out now from all the good things we have been doing."

Mr J.L.B. Matekoni chuckled. "In that case, you may have some sweets."

He handed a fistful of sweets over to the oldest child, who received them politely, with both hands extended, in the proper Botswana fashion.

"Do not spoil those children," shouted Mma Potokwane from her window. "They are very bad children, those ones."

The children laughed and scampered off, while Mr J.L.B. Matekoni walked through the office door. Inside, he found Mma Potokwane, her husband, who was a retired policeman, and a couple of the housemothers. Each had a mug of tea and a plate with a piece of fruit cake on it.

Mr J.L.B. Matekoni sipped on his tea as Mma Potokwane told him about the problems they were having with one of their borehole pumps. The pump was overheating after less than half an hour's use and they were worried that it would seize up altogether.

"Oil," said Mr J.L.B. Matekoni. "A pump without oil gets hot. There must be a leak. A broken seal or something like that."

"And then there are the brakes on the minibus," said Mr Potokwane. "They make a very bad noise now."

"Brake pads," said Mr J.L.B. Matekoni. "It's about time we replaced them. They get so much dust in them in this weather and it wears them down. I'll take a look, but you'll probably have to bring it into the garage for the work to be done."

They nodded, and the conversation moved to events at the orphan farm. One of the orphans had just been given a job and would be moving to Francistown to take it up. Another orphan had received a pair of running shoes from a Swedish donor who sent gifts from time to time. He was the best runner on the farm and now he would be able to enter in competitions. Then there was a silence, and Mma Potokwane looked expectantly at Mr J.L.B. Matekoni.

"I hear that you have some news," she said after a while. "I hear that you're getting married."

Mr J.L.B. Matekoni looked down at his shoes. They had told nobody, as far as he knew, but that would not be enough to stop news getting out in Botswana. It must have been his maid, he thought. She would have told one of the other maids and they would have spread it to their employers. Everybody would know now.

"I'm marrying Mma Ramotswe," he began. "She is …"

"She's the detective lady, isn't she?" said Mma Potokwane. "I have heard all about her. That will make life every exciting for you. You will be lurking about all the time. Spying on people."

Mr J.L.B. Matekoni drew in his breath. "I shall be doing no such thing," he said. "I am not going to be a detective. That is Mma Ramotswe's business."

Mma Potokwane seemed disappointed. But then, she brightened up. "You will be buying her a diamond ring, I suppose," she said. "An engaged lady these days must wear a diamond ring to show that she is engaged."

Mr J.L.B. Matekoni stared at her. "Is it necessary?" he asked.

"It is very necessary,' said Mma Potokwane. "If you read any of the magazines, you will see that there are advertisements for diamond rings. They say that they are for engagements."

Mr J.L.B. Matekoni was silent. Then: "Diamonds are rather expensive, aren't they?"

"Very expensive," said one of the housemothers. "One thousand pula for a tiny, tiny diamond."

"More than that," said Mr Potokwane. "Some diamonds cost two hundred thousand pula. Just one diamond."

Mr J.L.B. Matekoni looked despondent. He was not a mean man, and was as generous with presents as he was with his time, but he was against any waste of money and it seemed to him that to spend that much on a diamond, even for a special occasion, was entirely wasteful.

"I shall speak to Mma Ramotswe about it," he said firmly, to bring the awkward topic to a close. "Perhaps she does not believe in diamonds."

"No," said Mma Potokwane. "She will believe in diamonds. All ladies believe in diamonds. That is one thing on which all ladies agree."

Mr J.L.B. Matekoni crouched down and looked at the pump. After he had finished tea with Mma Potokwane, he had followed the path that led to the pump house. It was one of those peculiar paths that seemed to wander, but which eventually reached its destination. This path made a lazy loop round some pumpkin fields before it dipped through a *donga*, a deep eroded ditch, and ended up in front of the small lean-to that protected the pump. The pump-house was itself shaded by a stand of umbrella-like thorn trees, which, when Mr J.L.B. Matekoni arrived, provided a welcome circle of shade. A tin-roofed shack, like the pump-house was, could become impossibly hot in the direct rays of the sun and that would not help any machinery inside.

Mr J.L.B. Matekoni put down his tool box at the entrance to the pump-house and cautiously pushed the door open. He was careful about places like this because they were very well suited for snakes. Snakes seemed to like machinery, for some reason, and he had more than once discovered a somnolent snake curled around a part of some machine on which he was working. Why they did it, he had no idea; it might have been something to do with warmth and motion. Did snakes dream about some good place for snakes? Did they think

that there was a heaven for snakes somewhere, where everything was down at ground level and there was nobody to
tread on them?

His eyes took a few moments to accustom themselves to
the dark of the interior, but after a while he saw that there
was nothing untoward inside. The pump was driven by a
large flywheel which was powered by an antiquated diesel
engine. Mr J.L.B. Matekoni sighed. This was the trouble.
Old diesel engines were generally reliable, but there came a
point in their existence when they simply had to be pensioned
off. He had hinted at this to Mma Potokwane, but she had
always come up with reasons why money should be spent on
other, more pressing projects.

"But water is the most important thing of all," said Mr
J.L.B. Matekoni. "If you can't water your vegetables, then
what are the children going to eat?"

"God will provide," said Mma Potokwane calmly. "He
will send us a new engine one day."

"Maybe," said Mr J.L.B. Matekoni. "But then maybe not.
God is sometimes not very interested in engines. I fix cars for
quite a few ministers of religion, and they all have trouble.
God's servants are not very good drivers."

Now, confronted with the evidence of diesel mortality, he
retrieved his tool box, extracted an adjustable spanner, and
began to remove the engine casing. Soon he was completely
absorbed in his task, like a surgeon above the anaesthetised
patient, stripping the engine to its solid, metallic heart. It
had been a fine engine in its day, the product of a factory
somewhere unimaginably far away – a loyal engine, an engine of character. Every engine seemed to be Japanese these
days, and made by robots. Of course these were reliable, because the parts were so finely turned and so obedient, but for
a man like Mr J.L.B. Matekoni those engines were as bland
as sliced white bread. There was nothing in them, no rough-

age, no idiosyncracies. And as a result, there was no challenge in fixing a Japanese engine.

He had often thought how sad it was that the next generation of mechanics might never have to fix one of these old engines. They were all trained to fix the modern engines which needed computers to find out their troubles. When somebody came in to the garage with a new Mercedes Benz, Mr J.L.B. Matekoni's heart sank. He could no longer deal with such cars as he had none of these new diagnostic machines that one needed. Without such a machine, how could he tell if a tiny silicon chip in some inaccessible part of the engine was sending out the wrong signal? He felt tempted to say that such drivers should get a computer to fix their car, not a live mechanic, but of course he did not, and he would do his best with the gleaming expanse of steel which nestled under the bonnets of such cars. But his heart was never in it.

Mr J.L.B. Matekoni had now removed the pump engine's cylinder heads and was peering into the cylinders themselves. It was exactly what he had imagined; they were both coked up and would need a rebore before too long. And when the pistons themselves were removed he saw that the rings were pitted and worn, as if affected by arthritis. This would affect the engine's efficiency drastically, which meant wasted fuel and less water for the orphans' vegetables. He would have to do what he could. He would replace some of the engine seals to staunch the oil loss and he would arrange for the engine to be brought in some time for a rebore. But there would come a time when none of this would help, and he thought they would then simply have to buy a new engine.

There was a sound behind him, and he was startled. The pump-house was a quiet place, and all that he had heard so far was the call of birds in the acacia trees. This was a human noise. He looked round, but there was nothing. Then it came again, drifting through the bush, a squeaking noise as if from an unoiled wheel. Perhaps one of the orphans was wheeling a wheelbarrow or pushing one of those toy cars which children liked to fashion out of bits of old wire and tin.

Mr J.L.B. Matekoni wiped his hands on a piece of rag and stuffed the rag back into his pocket. The noise seemed to be coming closer now, and then he saw it, emerging from the scrub bush that obscured the twists of the path: a wheelchair, in which a girl was sitting, propelling the chair herself. When she looked up from the path ahead of her and saw Mr J.L.B. Matekoni she stopped, her hands gripping the rims of the wheels. For a moment they stared at one another, and then she smiled and began to make her way over the last few yards of pathway.

She greeted him politely, as a well-brought-up child would do.

"I hope that you are well, Rra," she said, offering her right hand while her left hand laid across the forearm in a gesture of respect.

They shook hands.

"I hope that my hands are not too oily," said Mr J.L.B. Matekoni. "I have been working on the pump."

The girl nodded. "I have brought you some water, Rra. Mma Potokwane said that you had come out here without anything to drink and you might be thirsty."

She reached into a bag that was slung under the seat of the chair and extracted a bottle.

Mr J.L.B. Matekoni took the water gratefully. He had just begun to feel thirsty and was regretting his failure to bring water with him. He took a swig from the bottle, watching the girl as she drank. She was still very young – about eleven or twelve, he thought – and she had a pleasant, open face. Her hair had been braided, and there were beads worked into the knots. She wore a faded-blue dress, almost bleached to white by repeated washings, and a pair of scruffy *tackies* on her feet.

"Do you live here?' he asked. "On the farm?"

She nodded. "I have been here nearly one year," she answered. "I am here with my young brother. He is only five."

"Where did you come from?"

She lowered her gaze. "We came from up near Francistown. My mother is late. She died three years ago, when I was nine. We lived with a woman, in her yard. Then she told us we had to go."

Mr J.L.B. Matekoni said nothing. Mma Potokwane had told him the stories of some of the orphans, and each time he found that it made his heart smart with pain. In traditional society there was no such thing as an unwanted child; everybody would be looked after by somebody. But things were changing, and now there were orphans. This was particularly so now that there was this disease which was stalking through Africa. There were many more children now without parents and the orphan farm might be the only place for some of them to go. Is this what had happened to this girl? And why was she in a wheelchair?

He stopped his line of thought. There was no point in speculating about things which one could do little to help. There were more immediate questions to be answered, such as why was the wheelchair making such an odd noise.

"Your chair is squeaking,' he said. "Does it always do that?"

She shook her head. "It started a few weeks ago. I think there is something wrong with it."

Mr J.L.B. Matekoni went down on his haunches and examined the wheels. He had never fixed a wheelchair before, but it was obvious to him what the problem was. The bearings were dry and dusty – a little oil would work wonders there – and the brake was catching. That would explain the noise.

"I shall lift you out," he said. "You can sit under the tree while I fix this chair for you."

He lifted the girl and placed her gently on the ground. Then, turning the chair upside down, he freed the brake block and readjusted the lever which operated it. Oil was applied to the bearings and the wheels were spun experimentally. There was no obstruction, and no noise. He righted the chair and pushed it over to where the girl was sitting.

"You have been very kind, Rra," she said. "I must get back now, or the House Mother will think I'm lost."

She made her way down the path, leaving Mr J.L.B. Matekoni to his work on the pump. He continued with the repair and after an hour it was ready. He was pleased when it started first time and appeared to run reasonably sweetly. The repair, however, would not last for long, and he knew that he would have to return to dismantle it completely. And how would the vegetables get water then? This was the trouble with living in a dry country. Everything, whether it was human life, or pumpkins, was on such a tiny margin.

CHAPTER FIVE

Judgment-day Jewellers

MMA POTOKWANE WAS right: Mma Ramotswe was, as she had predicted, interested in diamonds.

The subject came up a few days after Mr J.L.B. Matekoni had fixed the pump at the orphan farm.

"I think that people know that about engagement," said Mma Ramotswe, as she and Mr J.L.B. Matekoni sat drinking tea in the office of Tlokweng Road Speedy Motors. "My maid said that she had heard people talking about it in the town. She said that everybody knows."

"That is what this place is like," sighed Mr J.L.B. Matekoni. "I am always hearing about other people's secrets."

Mma Ramotswe nodded. He was right: there were no secrets in Gaborone. Everybody knew everybody else's business.

"For example," said Mr J.L.B. Matekoni, warming to the theme. "When Mma Sonqkwena ruined the gearbox of her son's new car by trying to change into reverse at thirty miles an hour, everybody seemed to hear about that. I told nobody, but they seemed to find out all the same."

Mma Ramotswe laughed. She knew Mma Sonqkwena, who was possibly the oldest driver in town. Her son, who had a profitable store in the Broadhurst Mall, had tried to persuade his mother to employ a driver or to give up driving altogether, but had been defeated by her indomitable sense of independence.

"She was heading out to Molepolole," went on Mr J.L.B. Matekoni, "and she remembered that she had not fed the chickens back in Gaborone. So she decided that she would go straight back by changing into reverse. You can imagine what that did to the gearbox. And suddenly everybody was talking about it. They assumed that I had told people, but I hadn't. A mechanic should be like a priest. He should not talk about what he sees."

Mma Ramotswe agreed. She appreciated the value of confidentiality, and she admired Mr J.L.B. Matekoni for understanding this too. There were far too many loose-tongued people about. But these were general observations, and there were more pressing matters still to be discussed, and so she brought the conversation round to the subject which had started the whole debate.

"So they are talking about our engagement," she said. "Some of them even asked to see the ring you had bought me." She glanced at Mr J.L.B. Matekoni before continuing. "So I told them that you hadn't bought it yet but that I'm sure that you would be buying it soon."

She held her breath. Mr J.L.B. Matekoni was looking at the ground, as he often did when he felt uncertain.

"A ring?" he said at last, his voice strained. "What kind of ring?"

Mma Ramotswe watched him carefully. One had to be circumspect with men, when discussing such matters. They had very little understanding of them, of course, but one had to be careful not to alarm them. There was no point in doing that. She decided to be direct. Mr J.L.B. Matekoni would spot subterfuge and it would not help.

"A diamond ring,' she said. "That is what engaged ladies are wearing these days. It is the modern thing to do."

Mr J.L.B. Matekoni continued to look glumly at the ground.

"Diamonds?" he said weakly. "Are you sure this is the most modern thing?"

"Yes," said Mma Ramotswe firmly. "All engaged ladies in modern circles receive diamond rings these days. It is a sign that they are appreciated."

Mr J.L.B. Matekoni looked up sharply. If this was true –
and it very much accorded with what Mma Potokwane had
told him – then he would have no alternative but to buy a
diamond ring. He would not wish Mma Ramotswe to imagine that she was not appreciated. He appreciated her greatly;
he was immensely, humbly grateful to her for agreeing to
marry him, and if a diamond were necessary to announce
that to the world, then that was a small price to pay. He
halted as the word "price" crossed his mind, recalling the
alarming figures which had been quoted over tea at the orphan farm.

"These diamonds are very expensive,' he ventured. "I hope
that I shall have enough money."

"But of course you will," said Mma Ramotswe. "They
have some very inexpensive ones. Or you can get terms …"

Mr J.L.B. Matekoni perked up, "I thought that they cost
thousands and thousands of pula," he said. "Maybe fifty
thousand pula."

"Of course not," said Mma Ramotswe. "They have expensive ones, of course, but they also have very good ones
that do not cost too much. We can go and take a look. Judgment-day Jewellers, for example. They have a good selection."

The decision was made. The next morning, after Mma
Ramotswe had dealt with the mail at the detective agency,
they would go to Judgment-day Jewellers and choose a ring.
It was an exciting prospect, and even Mr J.L.B. Matekoni,
feeling greatly relieved at the prospect of an affordable ring,
found himself looking forward to the outing. Now that he
had thought about it, there was something very appealing
about diamonds, something that even a man could understand, if only he were to think hard enough about it. What
was more important to Mr J.L.B. Matekoni was the thought
that this gift, which was possibly the most expensive gift he

would ever give in his life, was a gift from the very soil of Botswana. Mr J.L.B. Matekoni was a patriot. He loved his country, just as he knew Mma Ramotswe did. The thought that the diamond which he eventually chose could well have come from one of Botswana's own three diamond mines added to the significance of the gift. He was giving, to the woman whom he loved and admired more than any other, a tiny speck of the very land on which they walked. It was a special speck of course: a fragment of rock which had been burned to a fine point of brightness all those years ago. Then somebody had dug it out of the earth up at Orapa, polished it, brought it down to Gaborone, and set it in gold. And all of this to allow Mma Ramotswe to wear it on the second finger of her left hand and announce to the world that he, Mr J.L.B. Matekoni, the proprietor of Tlokweng Road Speedy Motors, was to be her husband.

The premises of Judgment-day Jewellers were tucked away at the end of a dusty street, alongside the Salvation Bookshop, which sold Bibles and other religious texts, and Mothobani Bookkeeping Services: *Tell the Taxman to go away*. It was a rather unprepossessing shop, with a sloping verandah roof supported by white-washed brick pillars. The sign, which had been painted by an amateur sign-writer of modest talent, showed the head and shoulders of a glamorous woman wearing an elaborate necklace and large pendant ear-rings. The woman was smiling in a lop-sided way, in spite of the weight of the ear-rings and the evident discomfort of the necklace.

Mr J.L.B. Matekoni and Mma Ramotswe parked on the opposite side of the road, under the shade of an acacia tree. They were later than they had anticipated, and the heat of the day was already beginning to build up. By mid-day any vehicle left out in the sun would be almost impossible to touch, the seats too hot for exposed flesh, the steering wheel a rim of fire. Shade would prevent this, and under every tree there were nests of cars, nosed up against the trunks, like piglets to a sow, in order to enjoy the maximum protection afforded by the incomplete panoply of grey-green foliage.

The door was locked, but clicked open obligingly when Mr J.L.B. Matekoni sounded the electric bell. Inside the shop, standing behind the counter, was a thin man clad in khaki. He had a narrow head, and both his slightly slanted eyes and the golden tinge to his skin suggested some San blood – the blood of the Kalahari bushmen. But if this were so, then what would he be doing working in a jewellery shop? There was no real reason why he should not, of course, but it seemed inappropriate. Jewellery shops attracted Indian people, or Kenyans, who liked work of that sort; Basarwa were happier working with livestock – they made great cattlemen or ostrich hands.

The jeweller smiled at them. "I saw you outside," he said. "You parked your car under that tree."

Mr J.L.B. Matekoni knew that he was right. The man spoke correct Setswana, but his accent confirmed the visible signs. Underneath the vowels, there were clicks and whistles struggling to get out. It was a peculiar language, the San language, more like the sound of birds in the trees than people talking.

He introduced himself, as was polite, and then he turned to Mma Ramotswe.

"This lady is now engaged to me," he said. "She is Mma Ramotswe, and I wish to buy her a ring for this engagement." He paused. "A diamond ring."

The jeweller looked at him through his hooded eyes, and then shifted his gaze sideways to Mma Ramotswe. She looked back at him, and thought: *There is intelligence here. This is a clever man who cannot be trusted.*

[49]

"You are a fortunate man," said the jeweller. "Not every man can find such a cheerful, fat woman to marry. There are many thin, hectoring women around today. This one will make you very happy."

Mr J.L.B. Matekoni acknowledged the compliment. "Yes," he said. "I am a lucky man."

"And now you must buy her a very big ring," went on the jeweller. "A fat woman cannot wear a tiny ring."

Mr J.L.B. Matekoni looked down at his shoes.

"I was thinking of a medium-sized ring," he said. "I am not a rich man."

"I know who you are," said the jeweller. "You are the man who owns Tlokweng Road Speedy Motors. You can afford a good ring."

Mma Ramotswe decided to intervene. "I do not want a big ring," she said firmly. "I am not a lady to wear a big ring. I was hoping for a small ring."

The jeweller threw her a glance. He seemed almost annoyed by her presence – as if this were a transaction between men, like a transaction over cattle, and she was interfering.

"I'll show you some rings," he said, bending down to slide a drawer out of the counter below him. "Here are some good diamond rings."

He placed the drawer on the top of the counter and pointed to a row of rings nestling in velvet slots. Mr J.L.B. Matekoni caught his breath. The diamonds were set in the rings in clusters: a large stone in the middle surrounded by smaller ones. Several rings had other stones too – emeralds and rubies – and beneath each of them a small tag disclosed.

"Don't pay any attention to what the label says," said the jeweller, lowering his voice. "I can offer very big discounts."

Mma Ramotswe peered at the tray. Then she looked up and shook her head.

"These are too big," she said. "I told you that I wanted a

smaller ring. Perhaps we shall have to go to some other shop."

The jeweller sighed. "I have some others," he said. "I have small rings as well."

He slipped the tray back into its place and extracted another. The rings on this one were considerably smaller. Mma Ramotswe pointed to a ring in the middle of the tray.

"I like that one," she said. "Let us see that one."

"It is not very big," said the jeweller. "A diamond like that may easily be missed. People may not notice it."

"I don't care," said Mma Ramotswe. "This diamond is going to be for me. It is nothing to do with other people."

Mr J.L.B. Matekoni felt a surge of pride as she spoke. This was the woman he admired, the woman who believed in the old Botswana values and who had no time for showiness.

"I like that ring too," he said. "Please let Mma Ramotswe try it on."

The ring was passed to Mma Ramotswe, who slipped it on her finger and held out her hand for Mr J.L.B. Matekoni to examine.

"It suits you perfectly," he said.

She smiled. "If this is the ring you would like to buy me, then I would be very happy."

The jeweller picked up the price tag and passed it to Mr J.L.B. Matekoni. "There can be no further discount on this one," he said. "It is already very cheap."

Mr J.L.B. Matekoni was pleasantly surprised by the price. He had just replaced the coolant unit on a customer's van and this, he noticed, was the same price, down to the last pula. It was not expensive. Reaching into his pocket, he took out the wad of notes which he had drawn from the bank earlier that morning and paid the jeweller.

"One thing I must ask you," Mr J.L.B. Matekoni said to the jeweller. "Is this diamond a Botswana diamond?"

The jeweller looked at him curiously.

"Why are you interested in that?' he asked. "A diamond is a diamond wherever it comes from."

"I know that," said Mr J.L.B. Matekoni. "But I would like to think that my wife will be wearing one of our own stones."

The jeweller smiled. "In that case, yes, it is. All these stones are stones from our own mines."

"Thank you," said Mr J.L.B. Matekoni. "I am happy to hear that."

They drove back from the jeweller's shop, past the Anglican Cathedral and the Princess Marina Hospital. As they passed the Cathedral, Mma Ramotswe said: "I think that perhaps we should get married there. Perhaps we can get Bishop Makhulu himself to marry us."

"I would like that," said Mr J.L.B. Matekoni. "He is a good man, the Bishop."

"Then a good man will be conducting the wedding of a good man," said Mma Ramotswe. "You are a kind man, Mr J.L.B. Matekoni."

Mr J.L.B. Matekoni said nothing. It was not easy to respond to a compliment, particularly when one felt that the compliment was undeserved. He did not think that he was a particularly good man. There were many faults in his character, he thought, and if anyone was good, it was Mma Ramotswe. She was far better than he was. He was just a mechanic who tried his best; she was far more than that.

They turned down Zebra Drive and drove into the short drive in front of Mma Ramotswe's house, bringing the car to a halt under the shade-netting at the side of her verandah. Rose, Mma Ramotswe's maid, looked out of the kitchen window and waved to them. She had done the day's laundry and it was hanging out on the line, white against the red-brown earth and blue sky.

Mr J.L.B. Matekoni took Mma Ramotswe's hand, touching, for a moment, the glittering ring. He looked at her, and saw that there were tears in her eyes.

"I'm sorry," she said. "I should not be crying, but I cannot help it."

"Why are you sad?" he asked. "You must not be sad."

She wiped away a tear and the shook her head.

"I'm not sad," she said. "It's just that nobody has ever given me anything like this ring before. When I married Note he gave me nothing. I had hoped that there would be a ring, but there was not. Now I have a ring."

"I will try to make up for Note," said Mr J.L.B. Matekoni. "I will try to be a good husband for you."

Mma Ramotswe nodded. "You will be," she said. "And I shall try to be a good wife for you."

They sat for a moment, saying nothing, each with the thoughts that the moment demanded. Then Mr J.L.B. Matekoni got out, walked round the front of the car, and opened her door for her. They would go inside for bush tea and she would show Rose the ring and the diamond that had made her so happy and so sad at the same time.

CHAPTER SIX

A Dry Place

SITTING IN HER office at the No. 1 Ladies' Detective Agency,
Mma Ramotswe reflected on how easy it was to find oneself committed to a course of action simply because one lacked
the courage to say no. She did not really want to take on the
search for a solution to what happened to Mrs Curtin's son;
Clovis Andersen, the author of her professional bible, *The
Principles of Private Detection*, would have described the
enquiry as stale. "A stale enquiry," he wrote, "is unreward-
ing to all concerned. The client is given false hopes because a
detective is working on the case, and the agent himself feels
committed to coming up with something because of the client's expectations. This means that the agent will probably
spend more time on the case than the circumstances should
warrant. At the end of the day, nothing is likely to be achieved
and one is left wondering whether there is not a case for
allowing the past to be buried with decency. *Let the past
alone* is sometimes the best advice that can be given."

Mma Ramotswe had re-read this passage several times
and had found herself agreeing with the sentiments it expressed. There was far too much interest in the past, she
thought. People were forever digging up events that had tak-
en place a long time ago. And what was the point in doing
this if the effect was merely to poison the present? There
were many wrongs in the past, but did it help to keep bringing them up and giving them a fresh airing? She thought of
the Shona people and how they kept going on about what
the Ndebele did to them under Mzilikazi and Lobengula. It
is true that they did terrible things – after all, they were real-

[54]

ly Zulus and had always oppressed their neighbours – but surely that was no justification for continuing to talk about it. It would be better to forget all that once and for all.

She thought of Seretse Khama, Paramount Chief of the Bamgwato, First President of Botswana, Statesman. Look at the way the British had treated him, refusing to recognize his choice of bride and forcing him into exile simply because he had married an Englishwoman. How could they have done such an insensitive and cruel thing to a man like that? To send a man away from his land, from his people, was surely one of the cruellest punishments that could be devised. And it left the people leaderless; it cut at their very soul: *Where is our Khama? Where is the son of Kgosi Sekgoma II and the mohumagadi Tebogo?* But Seretse himself never made much of this later on. He did not talk about it and he was never anything but courteous to the British Government and to the Queen herself. A lesser man would have said: Look what you did to me, and now you expect me to be your friend!

Then there was Mr Mandela. Everybody knew about Mr Mandela and how he had forgiven those who had imprisoned him. They had taken away years and years of his life simply because he wanted justice. They had set him to work in a quarry and his eyes had been permanently damaged by the rock dust. But at last, when he had walked out of the prison on that breathless, luminous day, he had said nothing about revenge or even retribution. He had said that there were more important things to do than to complain about the past, and in time he had shown that he meant this by hundreds of acts of kindness towards those who had treated him so badly. That was the real African way, the tradition that was closest to the heart of Africa. We are all children of Africa, and none of us is better or more important that the other. This is what Africa could say to the world: it could remind it what it is to be human.

[55]

She appreciated that, and she understood the greatness that Khama and Mandela showed in forgiving the past. And yet, Mrs Curtin's case was different. It did not seem to her that the American woman was keen to find somebody to blame for her son's disappearance, although she knew that there were many people in such circumstances who became obsessed with finding somebody to punish. And, of course, there was the whole problem of punishment. Mma Ramotswe sighed. She supposed that punishment was sometimes needed to make it clear that what somebody had done was wrong, but she had never been able to understand why we should wish to punish those who repented for their misdeeds. When she was a girl in Mochudi, she had seen a boy beaten for losing a goat. He had confessed that he had gone to sleep under a tree when he should have been watching the herd, and he had said that he was truly sorry that he had allowed the goat to wander. What was the point, she wondered, in his uncle beating him with a mopani stick until he cried out for mercy? Such punishment achieved nothing and merely disfigured the person who exacted it.

But these were large issues, and the more immediate problem was where to start with the search for that poor, dead American boy. She imagined Clovis Andersen shaking his head and saying, "Well, Mma Ramotswe, you've landed yourself with a stale case in spite of what I say about these things. But since you've done so, then my usual advice to you is to go back to the beginning. Start there." The beginning, she supposed, was the farm where Burkhardt and his friends had set up their project. It would not be difficult to find the place itself, although she doubted whether she would discover anything. But at least it would give her a feeling for the matter, and that, she knew, was the beginning. Places had echoes - and if one were sensitive, one might just pick up some resonance from the past, some feeling for what had happened.

At least she knew how to find the village. Her secretary, Mma Makutsi, had a cousin who came from the village nearest to the farm and she had explained which road to take. It was out to the west, not far from Molepolole. It was dry country, verging on the Kalahari, covered with low bushes and thorn trees. It was sparsely populated, but in those areas where there was more water, people had established small villages and clusters of small houses around the sorghum and melon fields. There was not much to do here, and people moved to Lobatse or Gaborone for work if they were in a position to do so. Gaborone was full of people from places like this. They came to the city, but kept their ties with their lands and their cattle post. Places like this would always be home, no matter how long people spent away. At the end of the day, this is where they would wish to die, under these great, wide skies, which were like a limitless ocean.

She travelled down in her tiny white van on a Saturday morning, setting off early, as she liked to do on any trip. As she left the town, there were already streams of people coming in for a Saturday's shopping. It was the end of the month, which meant pay day, and the shops would be noisy and crowded as people bought their large jars of syrup and beans, or splashed out on the coveted new dress or shoes. Mma Ramotswe liked shopping, but she never shopped around pay day. Prices went up then, she was convinced, and went down again towards the middle of the month, when nobody had any money.

Most of the traffic on the road consisted of buses and vans bringing people in. But there were a few going in the opposite direction – workers from town heading off for a weekend back in their villages; men going back to their wives and children; women working as maids in Gaborone going back to spend their precious days of leisure with their parents and grandparents. Mma Ramotswe slowed down; there was a woman standing at the side of the road, waving her hand to request a lift. She was a woman of about Mma Ramotswe's age, dressed smartly in a black skirt and a bright-red jersey. Mma Ramotswe hesitated, and then stopped. She could not leave her standing there; somewhere there would be a family waiting for her, counting on a motorist to bring their mother home.

She drew to a halt, and called out of the window of her van. "Where are you going, Mma?"

"I am going down that way," said the woman, pointing down the road. "Just beyond Molepolole. I am going to Silokwolela."

Mma Ramotswe smiled. "I am going there too," she said. "I can take you all the way."

The woman let out a whoop of delight. "You are very kind, and I am a very lucky person."

She reached down for the plastic bag in which she was carrying her possessions and opened the passenger door of Mma Ramotswe's van. Then, her belongings stored at her feet, Mma Ramotswe pulled out into the road again and they set off. From old habit, Mma Ramotswe glanced at her new travelling companion and made her assessment. She was quite well dressed – the jersey was new, and was real wool rather than the cheap artificial fibres that so many people bought these days; the skirt was a cheap one, though, and the shoes were slightly scuffed. This lady works in a shop, she thought. She has passed her standard six, and maybe even form two or three. She has no husband, and her children are living with the grandmother out at Silokwolela. Mma Ramotswe had seen the copy of the Bible tucked into the top of the plastic bag and this had given her more information. This lady was a member of a church, and was perhaps going to bible classes. She would be reading her Bible to the children that night.

"Your children are down there, Mma?" asked Mma Ramotswe politely.

"Yes," came the reply. "They are staying with their grandmother. I work in a shop in Gaborone, New Deal Furnishers. You know them maybe?"

Mma Ramotswe nodded, as much for the confirmation of her judgement as in answer to the question.

"I have no husband," she went on. "He went to Francistown and he died of burps."

Mma Ramotswe gave a start. "Burps? You can die of burps?"

"Yes. He was burping very badly up in Francistown and they took him to the hospital. They gave him an operation and they found that there was something very bad inside him. This thing made him burp. Then he died."

There was a silence. Then Mma Ramotswe spoke. "I am very sorry."

"Thank you. I was very sad when this happened, as he was a very good man and he had been a good father to my children. But my mother was still strong, and she said that she would look after them. I could get a job in Gaborone, because I have my form two certificate. I went to the furniture shop and they were very pleased with my work. I am now one of the top salesladies and they have even booked me to go on a sales training course in Mafikeng."

Mma Ramotswe smiled. "You have done very well. It is not easy for women. Men expect us to do all the work and then they take the best jobs. It is not easy to be a successful lady."

"But I can tell that you are successful," said the woman. "I can tell that you are a business lady. I can tell that you are doing well."

Mma Ramotswe thought for a moment. She prided herself on her ability to sum people up, but she wondered whether this was not something that many women had, as part of the intuitive gift.

"You tell me what I do," she said. "Could you guess what my job is?"

The woman turned in her seat and looked Mma Ramotswe up and down.

"You are a detective, I think," she said. "You are a person who looks into other people's business."

The tiny white van swerved momentarily. Mma Ramotswe was shocked that this woman had guessed. Her intuitive powers must be even better than mine, she thought.

"How did you know that? What did I do to give you this information."

The other woman shifted her gaze. "It was simple," she said. "I have seen you sitting outside your detective agency drinking tea with your secretary. She is that lady with very big glasses. The two of you sit there in the shade sometimes and I have been walking past on the other side of the road. That is how I knew."

They travelled in comfortable companionship, talking about their daily lives. She was called Mma Tsbago, and she told Mma Ramotswe about her work in the furniture shop. The manager was a kind man, she said, who did not work his staff too hard and who was always honest with his customers. She had been offered a job by another firm, at a higher wage, but had refused it. Her manager found out and had rewarded her loyalty with a promotion.

Then there were her children. They were a girl of ten and a boy of eight. They were doing well at school and she hoped that she might be able to bring them to Gaborone for their secondary education. She had heard the Gaborone Government Secondary School was very good and she hoped that she might be able to get a place for them there. She had also heard that there were scholarships to even better schools, and perhaps they might have a chance of one of those.

Mma Ramotswe told her that she was engaged to be married, and she pointed to the diamond on her finger. Mma Tsbago admired it and asked who the fiancé was. It was a good thing to marry a mechanic, she said, as she had heard that they made the best husbands. You should try to marry a policeman, a mechanic or a minister of religion, she said, and you should never marry a politician, a barman, or a taxi driver. These people always caused a great deal of trouble for their wives.

"And you shouldn't marry a trumpeter," added Mma Ramotswe. "I made that mistake. I married a bad man called Note Mokoti. He played the trumpet."

"I'm sure that they are not good people to marry," said Mma Tsbago. "I shall add them to my list."

They made slow progress on the last part of the journey. The road, which was untarred, was pitted with large and dangerous pot-holes, and at several points they were obliged to edge dangerously out into the sandy verge to avoid a particularly large hole. This was perilous, as the tiny white van could easily become stuck in the sand if they were not careful and they might have to wait hours for rescue. But at last they arrived at Mma Tsbago's village, which was the village closest to the farm that Mma Ramotswe was seeking.

She had asked Mma Tsbago about the settlement, and had been provided with some information. She remembered the project, although she had not known the people involved in it. She recalled that there had been a white man and a woman from South Africa, and one or two other foreigners. A number of the people from the village had worked there, and people had thought that great things would come of it, but it had eventually fizzled out. She had not been surprised at that. Things fizzled out; you could not hope to change Africa. People lost interest, or they went back to their traditional way of doing things, or they simply gave up because it was all too much effort. And then Africa had a way of coming back and simply covering everything up again.

"Is there somebody in the village who can take me out there?" asked Mma Ramotswe.

Mma Tsbago thought for a moment.

"There are still some people who worked out there," she said. "There is a friend of my uncle. He had a job out there for a while. We can go to his place and you can ask him."

They went first to Mma Tsbago's house. It was a traditional Botswana house, made out of ochre mud bricks and surrounded by a low wall, a lomotana, which created a tiny yard in front of and alongside the house. Outside this wall there were two thatched grain bins, on raised legs, and a chicken house. At the back, made out of tin and leaning dangerously, was the privy, with an old plank door and a rope with which the door could be tied shut. The children ran out immediately, and embraced their mother, before waiting shyly to be introduced to the stranger. Then, from the dark interior of the house, there emerged the grandmother, wearing a threadbare white dress and grinning toothlessly.

Mma Tsbago left her bag in the house and explained that she would return within an hour. Mma Ramotswe gave sweets to the children, which they received with both palms upturned, thanking her gravely in the correct Setswana manner. These were children who would understand the old ways, thought Mma Ramotswe, approvingly – unlike some of the children in Gaborone.

They left the house and drove through the village in the white van. It was a typical Botswana village a sprawling collection of one- or two- room houses, each in its own yard, each with a motley collection of thorn trees surrounding it. The houses were linked by paths, which wandered this way and that, skirting fields and crop patches. Cattle moved about listlessly, cropping at the occasional patch of brown, withered grass, while a pot-bellied herd-boy, dusty and be-aproned, watched them from under a tree. The cattle were unmarked, but everybody would know their owner, and their lineage. These were the signs of wealth, the embodied result of somebody's labours in the diamond mine at Jwaneng or the beef-canning factory at Lobatse.

Mma Tsbago directed her to a house on the edge of the village. It was a well-kept place, slightly larger than its immediate neighbours, and had been painted in the style of the traditional Botswana house, in reds and browns and with a bold, diamond pattern etched out in white. The yard was well-swept, which suggested that the woman of the house, who would also have painted it, was conscientious with her reed broom. Houses, and their decoration, were the responsibility of the woman, and this woman had evidently had the old skills passed down to her.

They waited at the gate while Mma Tsbago called out for permission to enter. It was rude to go up the path without first calling, and even ruder to go into a building uninvited.

"Ko, Ko!" called out Mma Tsbago. "Mma Potsane, I am here to see you!"

There was no response, and Mma Tsbago repeated her call. Again no answer came, and then the door of the house suddenly opened and a small, rotund woman, dressed in a long skirt and high-collared white blouse came out and peered in their direction.

"Who is that?" she called out, shading her eyes with a hand. "Who are you? I cannot see you."

"Mma Tsbago. You know me. I am here with a stranger."

The householder laughed. "I thought it might be somebody else, and I quickly got dressed up. But I need not have bothered!"

She gestured for them to enter and they walked across to meet her.

"I cannot see very well these days," explained Mma Potsane. "My eyes are getting worse and worse. That is why I didn't know who you were."

They shook hands, exchanging formal greetings. Then Mma Potsane gestured across to a bench which stood in the shade of the large tree beside her house. They could sit there, she explained, because the house was too dark inside.

Mma Tsbago explained why they were there and Mma Potsane listened intently. Her eyes appeared to be irritating her, and from time to time she wiped at them with the sleeve of her blouse. As Mma Tsbago spoke, she nodded encouragement.

"Yes," she said. "We lived out there. My husband worked there. We both worked there. We hoped that we would be able to make some money with our crops and for a while it worked. Then ..." She broke off, shrugging despondently.

"Things went wrong?" asked Mma Ramotswe. "Drought?"

Mma Potsane sighed. "There was a drought, yes. But there's always a drought, isn't there? No, it was just that people lost faith in the idea. There were good people living there, but they went away."

"The white man from Namibia? The German one?" asked Mma Ramotswe.

"Yes, that one. He was a good man, but he went away. Then there were other people, Batswana, who decided that they had had enough. They went too."

"And an American?" pressed Mma Ramotswe. "There was an American boy?"

Mma Potsane rubbed at her eyes. "That boy vanished.

He disappeared one night. They had the police out here and they searched and searched. His mother came too, many times. She brought a Mosarwa tracker with her, a tiny little man, like a dog with his nose to the ground. He had a very fat bottom, like all those Basarwa have."

"He found nothing?" Mma Ramotswe knew the answer to this, but she wanted to keep the other woman talking. She had so far only heard the story from Mrs Curtin's viewpoint; it was quite possible that there were things which other people had seen which she did not know about.

"He ran round and round like a dog," said Mma Potsane, laughing. "He looked under stones and sniffed the air and muttered away in that peculiar language of theirs – you know how it is, all those sounds like trees in the wind and twigs breaking. But he found no sign of any wild animals which may have taken that boy."

Mma Ramotswe passed her a handkerchief to dab her eyes. "So what do you think happened to him, Mma? How can somebody just vanish like that?"

Mma Potsane sniffed and then blew her nose on Mma Ramotswe's handkerchief.

"I think that he was sucked up," she said. "There are sometimes whirlwinds here in the very hot season. They come in from the Kalahari and they suck things up. I think that maybe that boy got sucked up in a whirlwind and put down somewhere far, far away. Maybe over by Ghanzi way or in the middle of the Kalahari or somewhere. No wonder they didn't find him."

Mma Tsbago looked sideways at Mma Ramotswe, trying to catch her eye, but Mma Ramotswe looked straight ahead at Mma Potsane.

"That is always possible, Mma," she said. "That is an interesting idea." She paused. "Could you take me out there and show me round? I have a van here."

Mma Potsane thought for a moment. "I do not like to go out there,' she said. "It is a sad place for me."

"I have twenty pula for your expenses,' said Mma Ramotswe, reaching into her pocket. "I had hoped that you would be able to accept this from me."

"Of course," said Mma Potsane hurriedly. "We can go there. I do not like to go there at night, but in the day it is different."

"Now?" said Mma Ramotswe. "Could you come now?"

"I am not busy," said Mma Potsane. "There is nothing happening here."

Mma Ramotswe passed the money over to Mma Potsane, who thanked her, clapping both hands in a sign of gratitude. Then they walked back over her neatly-swept yard and, saying goodbye to Mma Tsbago, they climbed into the van and drove off.

CHAPTER SEVEN

Further Problems with the Orphan-Farm Pump

O N THE DAY that Mma Ramotswe travelled out to Silok-wolela, Mr J.L.B. Matekoni felt vaguely ill at ease. He had been becomes accustomed to meeting Mma Ramotswe on a Saturday morning to help her with her shopping or with some task about the house. Without her, he felt at a loose end: Gaborone seemed strangely empty; the garage was closed, and he had no desire to attend to the paperwork that had been piling up on his desk. He could call on a friend, of course, and perhaps go and watch a football match, but again he was not in the mood for that. Then he thought of Mma Silvia Potokwane, Matron in Charge of the Orphan Farm. There was inevitably something happening out there, and she was always happy to sit down and have a chat over a cup of tea. He would go out there and see how everything was. Then the rest of the day could take care of itself until Mma Ramotswe returned that evening.

Mma Potokwane spotted him, as usual, as he parked his car under one of the syringa trees.

"I see you!" she shouted from her window. "I see you, Mr J.L.B. Matekoni!"

Mr J.L.B. Matekoni waved in her direction as he locked the car. Then he strode towards the office, where the sound of cheerful music drifted out of one of the windows. Inside, Mma Potokwane was sitting beside her desk, a telephone receiver to her ear. She motioned for him to sit down and continued with her conversation.

"If you can give me some of that cooking oil," she said, "the orphans will be very happy. They like to have their potatoes fried in oil and it is good for them."

The voice at the other end said something, and she frowned, glancing up at Mr J.L.B. Matekoni, as if to share her irritation.

"But you cannot sell that oil if it is beyond its expiry date. So why should I pay you anything for it? It would be better to give it to the orphans than to pour it down the drain. I cannot give you money for it, and so I see no reason why you shouldn't give it to us."

Again something was said on the other end of the line, and she nodded patiently.

"I can make sure that the *Daily News* comes to photograph you handing the oil over. Everybody will know that you are a generous man. It will be there in the papers."

There was a further brief exchange and then she replaced the receiver.

"Some people are slow to give,' she said. "It is something to do with how their mothers brought them up. I have read all about this problem in a book. There is a doctor called Dr Freud who is very famous and has written many books about such people."

"Is he in Johannesburg?" asked Mr J.L.B. Matekoni.

"I do not think so," said Mma Potokwane. "It is a book from London. But it is very interesting. He says that all boys are in love with their mother."

"That is natural," said Mr J.L.B. Matekoni. "Of course boys love their mothers. Why should they not do so?"

Mma Potokwane shrugged. "I agree with you. I cannot see what is wrong with a boy loving his mother."

"Then why is Dr Freud worried about this?" went on Mr J.L.B. Matekoni. "Surely he should be worried if they did *not* love their mothers."

Mma Potokwane looked thoughtful. "Yes. But he was still very worried about these boys and I think he tried to stop them."

"That is ridiculous," said Mr J.L.B. Matekoni. "Surely he had better things to do with his time."

"You would have thought so," said Mma Potokwane. "But in spite of this Dr Freud, boys still go on loving their mothers, which is how it should be."

She paused, and then, brightening at the abandonment of this difficult subject, she smiled broadly at Mr J.L.B. Matekoni. "I am very glad that you came out today. I was going to phone you."

Mr J.L.B. Matekoni sighed. "Brakes? Or the pump?"

"The pump," said Mma Potokwane. "It is making a very strange noise. The water comes all right, but the pump makes a noise as if it is in pain."

"Engines do feel pain," said Mr J.L.B. Matekoni. "They tell us of their pain by making a noise."

"Then this pump needs help," said Mma Potokwane. "Can you take a quick look at it?"

"Of course," said Mr J.L.B. Matekoni.

It took him longer than he had expected, but at last he found the cause and was able to attend to it. The pump reassembled, he tested it, and it ran sweetly once more. It would need a total refit, of course, and that day would not be able to be put off for much longer, but at least the strange, moaning sound had stopped.

Back in Mma Potokwane's office, he relaxed with his cup of tea and a large slab of currant cake which the cooks had baked that morning. The orphans were well fed. The Government looked after its orphans well and gave a generous grant each year. But there were also private donors – a network of people who gave in money, or kind, to the orphan farm. This meant that none of the orphans actually wanted for anything and none of them was malnourished, as happened in so many other African countries. Botswana was a well-blessed country. Nobody starved and nobody languished in prison for their political beliefs. As Mma Ramotswe had pointed out to him, the Batswana could hold their heads up anywhere – anywhere.

"This is good cake," said Mr J.L.B. Matekoni. "The children must love it."

Mma Potokwane smiled. "Our children love cake. If we gave them nothing but cake, they would be very happy. But of course we don't. The orphans needs onions and beans too."

Mr J.L.B. Matekoni nodded. "A balanced diet," he said widely. "They say that a balanced diet is the key to health."

There was silence for a moment as they reflected on his observation. Then Mma Potokwane spoke.

"So you will be a married man soon," she said. "That will make your life different. You will have to behave yourself, Mr J.L.B. Matekoni!"

He laughed, scraping up the last crumbs of his cake. "Mma Ramotswe will watch me. She will make sure that I behave myself well."

"Mmm," said Mma Potokwane. "Will you be living in her house or in yours?"

"I think it will be her house," said Mr J.L.B. Matekoni. "It is a bit nicer than mine. Her house is in Zebra Drive, you know."

"Yes," said the Matron. "I have seen her place. I drove past it the other day. It looks very nice."

Mr J.L.B. Matekoni looked surprised. "You drove past specially to take a look?"

"Well," said Mma Potokwane, grinning slightly. "I thought that I might just see what sort of place it was. It's quite big, isn't it?"

"It's a comfortable house," said Mr J.L.B. Matekoni. "I think that there will be enough room for us."

"Too much room," said Mma Potokwane. "There will be room for children."

Mr J.L.B. Matekoni frowned. "We had not been thinking of that. We are maybe a bit old for children. I am forty-five. And then ... Well, I do not like to talk about it, but Mma Ramotswe has told me that she cannot have children. She had a baby, you know, but it died and now the doctors have said to her that ..."

Mma Potokwane shook her head. "That is very sad. I am very sad for her."

"But we are very happy," said Mr J.L.B. Matekoni. "Even if we do not have children."

Mma Potokwane reached over to the teapot and poured her guest another cup of tea. Then she cut a further slice of cake – a generous helping – and slid it on to his plate.

"Of course, there is always adoption," she said, watching him as she spoke. "Or you could always just look after a child if you didn't want to adopt. You could take... " She paused, raising her teacup to her lips. "You could always take an orphan." Adding hurriedly: "Or even a couple of orphans."

Mr J.L.B. Matekoni stared at his shoes. "I don't know. I don't think I would like to adopt a child. But ... "

"But a child could come and live with you. There's no need to go to all the trouble of adoption papers and magistrates," said Mma Potokwane. "Imagine how nice that would be!"

"Maybe ... I don't know. Children are a big responsibility."

Mma Potokwane laughed. "But you're a man who takes responsibility easily. There you are with your garage, that's a responsibility. And those apprentices of yours. They're a responsibility too, aren't they? You are well used to responsibility."

Mr J.L.B. Matekoni thought of his apprentices. They, too,

had just appeared, sidling into the garage shortly after he had telephoned the technical trades college and offered to give two apprenticeships. He had entertained great hopes of them, but had been disappointed virtually from the beginning. When he was their age he had been full of ambition, but they seemed to take everything for granted. At first he had been unable to understand why they seemed so passive, but then all had been explained to him by a friend. "Young people these days cannot show enthusiasm," he had been told. "It's not considered smart to be enthusiastic." So this is what was wrong with the apprentices. They wanted to be thought smart.

On one occasion, when Mr J.L.B. Matekoni felt particularly irritated at seeing the two young men sitting unenthusiastically on their empty oil drums staring into the air he had raised his voice at them.

"So you think you're smart?" he shouted. "Is that what you think?"

The two apprentices had glanced at one another.

"No," said one, after a few moments. "No, we don't."

He had felt deflated and had slammed the door of his office. It appeared that they lacked the enthusiasm even to respond to his challenge, which just proved what he had thought anyway.

Now, thinking of children, he wondered whether he would have the energy to deal with them. He was approaching the point in life when he wanted a quiet and orderly time. He wanted to be able to fix engines in his own garage during the day and to spend his evenings with Mma Ramotswe. That would be bliss! Would children not introduce a note of stress into their domestic life? Children needed to be taken to school and put in the bathtub and taken to the nurse for injections. Parents always seemed so worn out by their children and he wondered whether he and Mma Ramotswe would really want that.

"I can tell that you're thinking about it," said Mma Potokwane. "I think your mind is almost made up."

"I don't know ..."

"What you should do is just take the plunge," she went on. "You could give the children to Mma Ramotswe as a wedding present. Women love children. She will be very pleased. She'll be getting a husband and some children all on the same day! Any lady would love that, believe me."

"But ..."

Mma Potokwane cut him short. "Now there are two children who would be very happy to go and live with you,' she said. "Let them come on trial. You can decide after a month or so whether they can stay."

"Two children? There are two?" stuttered Mr J.L.B. Matekoni. "I thought ... "

"They are a brother and sister," Mma Potokwane went on hurriedly. "We do not like to split up brothers and sisters. The girl is twelve and the boy is just five. They are very nice children."

"I don't know ... I would have to ..."

"In fact," said Mma Potokwane, rising to her feet. "I think that you have met one of them already. The girl who brought you water. The child who cannot walk."

Mr J.L.B. Matekoni said nothing. He remembered the child, who had been very polite and appreciative. But would it not be rather burdensome to look after a handicapped child? Mma Potokwane had said nothing about this when she had first raised the subject. She had slipped in an extra child – the brother – and now she was casually mentioning the wheel-chair, as if it made no difference. He stopped himself. He could be in that chair himself.

Mma Potokwane was looking out of the window. Now she turned to address him.

[73]

"Would you like me to call that child?' she asked. "I am not trying to force you, Mr J.L.B. Matekoni, but would you like to meet her again, and the little boy?"

The room was silent, apart from a sudden creak from the tin roof, expanding in the heat. Mr J.L.B. Matekoni looked down at his shoes, and remembered, for a moment, how it was to be a child, back in the village, all those years ago. And remembered how he had experienced the kindness of the local mechanic, who had let him polish trucks and help with the mending of punctures, and who by this kindness had revealed and nurtured a vocation. It was easy to make a difference to other people's lives, so easy to change the little room in which people lived their life.

"Call them," he said. "I would like to see them."

Mma Potokwane smiled. "You are a good man, Mr J.L.B. Matekoni," she said. "I will send word for them to come. They will have to be fetched from the fields. But while we are waiting, I'm going to tell you their story. You listen to this."

CHAPTER EIGHT

The Children's Tale

Y OU MUST UNDERSTAND, said Mma Potokwane, that although it is easy for us to criticize the ways of the Basarwa, we should think carefully before we do that. When
you look at the life they lead, out there in the Kalahari, with
no cattle of their own and no houses to live in; when you
think about that and wonder how long you and I and other
Batswana would be able to live like that, then you realize
that these bushmen are remarkable people.

There were some of these people who wandered around
on the edge of the Makadikadi Salt Pans, up on the road
over to the Okavango. I don't know that part of the country
very well, but I have been up there once or twice. I remember
the first time I saw it: a wide, white plain under a white sky,
with a few tall palm trees and grass that seemed to grow out
of nothing. It was such a strange landscape that I thought I
had wandered out of Botswana into some foreign land. But
just a little bit further on it changes back into Botswana and
you feel comfortable again.

There was a band of Masarwa who had come up from
the Kalahari to hunt ostriches. They must have found water
in the salt pans and then wandered on towards one of the
villages along the road to Maun. The people up there are
sometimes suspicious of Basarwa, as they say that they steal
their goats and will milk their cows at night if they are not
watched closely.

This band had made a camp about two or three miles
outside the village. They hadn't built anything, of course,
but were sleeping under the bushes, as they often do. They

had plenty of meat – having just killed several ostriches – and were happy to stay there until the urge came upon them to move.

There were a number of children and one of the women had just given birth to a baby, a boy. She was sleeping with him at her side, a little bit away form the others. She had a daughter, too, who was sleeping on the other side of her mother. The mother woke up, we assume, and moved her legs about to be more comfortable. Unfortunately there was a snake at her feet, and she rested her heel on its head. The snake bit her. That's how most snake bites occur. People are asleep on their sleeping mats and snakes come in for the warmth. Then they roll over on to the snake and the snake defends itself.

They gave her some of their herbs. They're always digging up roots and stripping bark off trees, but nothing like that can deal with a *lebolobolo* bite, which is what this must have been. According to the daughter, her mother died before the baby even woke up. Of course, they don't lose any time and they prepared to bury the mother that morning. But, as you might or might not know, Mr J.L.B. Matekoni, when a Mosarwa woman dies and she's still feeding a baby, they bury the baby too. There just isn't the food to support a baby without a mother. That's the way it is.

The girl hid in the bush and watched them take her mother and her baby brother. It was sandy there, and all they could manage was a shallow grave, in which they laid her mother, while the other women wailed and the men sang something. The girl watched as they put her tiny brother in the grave too, wrapped in an animal skin. Then they pushed the sand over them both and went back to the camp.

The moment they had gone, the child crept out and scrabbled quickly at the sand. It did not take her long, and soon she had her brother in her arms. There was sand in the child's nostrils, but he was still breathing. She turned on her heels and ran through the bush in the direction of the road, which she knew was not too far away. A truck came past a short time later, a Government truck from the Roads Department. The driver slowed, and then stopped. He must have been astonished to see a young Mosarwa child standing there with a baby in her arms. Of course he could hardly leave her, even though he could not make out what she was trying to tell him. He was going back to Francistown and he dropped her off at the Nyangabwe Hospital, handing her over to an orderly at the gate.

They looked at the baby, who was thin, and suffering badly from a fungal disease. The girl herself had tuberculosis, which is not at all unusual, and so they took her in and kept her in a TB ward for a couple of months while they gave her drugs. The baby stayed in the maternity nursery until the girl was better. Then, they let them go. Beds on the TB ward were needed for other sick people and it was not the hospital's job to look after a Mosarwa girl with a baby. I suppose they thought that she would go back to her people, which they usually do.

One of the sisters at the hospital was concerned. She saw the girl sitting at the hospital gate and she decided that she had nowhere to go. So she took her home and let her stay in her backyard, in a lean-to shack that they had used for storage but which could be cleared out to provide a room of sorts. This nurse and her husband fed the children, but they couldn't take them into the family properly, as they had two children of their own and they did not have a great deal of money.

The girl picked up Setswana quite quickly. She found ways of making a few pula by collecting empty bottles from the edge of the road and taking them back to the bottle store for the deposit. She carried the baby on her back, tied in a sling, and never let him leave her sight. I spoke to the nurse about her, and I understand that although she was still a child herself, she was a good mother to the boy. She made his clothes out of scraps that she found here and there, and she kept him clean by washing him under the tap in the nurse's backyard. Sometimes she would go and beg outside the railway station, and I think that people sometimes took pity on them and gave them money, but she preferred to earn it if she could.

This went on for four years. Then, quite without warning, the girl became ill. They took her back to the hospital and they found that the tuberculosis had damaged the bones very badly. Some of them had crumbled and this was making it difficult for her to walk. They did what they could, but they were unable to prevent her from ending up unable to walk. The nurse scrounged around for a wheelchair, which she was eventually given by one of the Roman Catholic priests. So now she looked after the boy from the wheelchair, and he, for his part, did little chores for his sister.

The nurse and her husband had to move. The husband worked for a meat-packing firm and they wanted him down in Lobatse. The nurse had heard of the orphan farm, and so she wrote to me. I said that we could take them, and I went up to Francistown to collect them just a few months ago. Now they are with us, as you have seen.

That is their story, Mr J.L.B. Matekoni. That is how they came to be here.

Mr J.L.B. Matekoni said nothing. He looked at Mma Potok-wane, who met his gaze. She had worked at the orphan farm for almost twenty years – she had been there when it had been started – and was inured to tragedy – or so she thought. But this story, which she had just told, had affected her profoundly when she had first heard it from the nurse in Francistown. Now it was having that effect on Mr J.L.B.

Matekoni as well; she could see that.

"They will be here in a few moments,' she said. "Do you want me to say that you might be prepared to take them?"

Mr J.L.B. Matekoni closed his eyes. He had not spoken to Mma Ramotswe about it and it seemed quite wrong to land her with something like this without consulting her first. Was this the way to start a marriage? To take a decision of such momentum without consulting one's spouse? Surely not.

And yet here were the children. The girl in her wheelchair, smiling up at him and the boy standing there so gravely, eyes lowered out of respect.

He drew in his breath. There were times in life when one had to act, and this, he suspected, was one of them.

"Would you children like to come and stay with me?" he said. "Just for a while? Then we can see how things go."

The girl looked to Mma Potokwane, as if for confirmation.

"Rra Matekoni will look after you well," she said. "You will be happy there."

The girl turned to her brother and said something to him, which the adults did not hear. The boy thought for moment, and then nodded.

"You are very kind, Rra," she said. "We will be very happy to come with you."

Mma Potokwane clapped her hands.

"Go and pack, children,' she said. "Tell your housemother that they are to give you clean clothes."

The girl turned her wheelchair round and left the room, accompanied by her brother.

"What have I done?" muttered Mr J.L.B. Matekoni, under his breath,

Mma Potokwane gave him his answer.

"A very good thing," she said.

CHAPTER NINE

The Wind Must Come from Somewhere

THEY DROVE OUT of the village in Mma Ramotswe's tiny white van. The dirt road was rough, virtually disappearing at points into deep pot-holes or rippling into a sea of corrugations that made the van creak and rattle in protest. The farm was only eight miles away from the village, but they made slow progress, and Mma Ramotswe was relieved to have Mma Potsane with her. It would be easy to get lost in the featureless bush, with no hills to guide one and each tree looking much like the next one. Though for Mma Potsane the landscape, even if dimly glimpsed, was rich in associations. Her eyes squeezed almost shut, she peered out of the van, pointing out the place where they had found a stray donkey years before, and there, by that rock, that was where a cow had died for no apparent reason. These were the intimate memories that made the land alive - that bound people to a stretch of baked earth, as valuable to them, and as beautiful, as if it were covered with sweet grass.

Mma Potsane sat forward in her seat. "There," she said. "Do you see it over there? I can see things better if they are far away. I can see it now."

Mma Ramotswe followed her gaze. The bush had become denser, thick with thorn trees, and these concealed, but not quite obscured, the shape of the buildings. Some of these were typical of the ruins to be found in southern Africa; white-washed walls that seemed to have crumbled until they were a few feet above the ground, as if flattened from above; others still had their roofs, or the framework of their roofs, the thatch having collapsed inwards, consumed by ants or taken by birds for nests.

"That is the farm?"

"Yes. And over there – do you see over there – that is where we lived."

It was a sad homecoming for Mma Potsane, as she had warned Mma Ramotswe; this was where she had spent that quiet time with her husband after he had spent all those years away in the mines in South Africa. Their children grown up, they had been thrown back on each other's company and enjoyed the luxury of an uneventful life.

"We did not have much to do," she said. "My husband went every day to work in the fields. I sat with the other women and made clothes. The German liked us to make clothes, which he would sell in Gaborone."

The road petered out, and Mma Ramotswe brought the van to a halt under a tree. Stretching her legs, she looked through the trees at the building which must have been the main house. There must have eleven or twelve houses at one time, judging from the ruins scattered about. It was so sad, she thought; all these buildings set down in the middle of the bush like this; all that hope, and now, all that remained were the mud foundations and the crumbling walls.

They walked over to the main house. Much of the roof had survived, as it, unlike the others, had been made of corrugated iron. There were doors too, old gauze-screened doors hanging off their jams, and glass in some of the windows.

"That is where the German lived," said Mma Potsane. "And the American and the South African woman, and some other people from far away. We Batswana lived over there."

Mma Ramotswe nodded. "I should like to go inside that house."

Mma Potsane shook her head. "There will be nothing," she said. "The house is empty. Everybody has gone away."

"I know that. But now that we have come out here, I

should like to see what it is like inside. You don't need to go in if you don't want to."

Mma Potsane winced. "I cannot let you go in by yourself," she muttered. "I shall come in with you."

They pushed at the screen which blocked the front doorway. The wood had been mined by termites, and it gave way at a touch.

"The ants will eat everything in this country," said Mma Potsane. "One day only the ants will be left. They will have eaten everything else."

They entered the house, feeling straight away the cool that came with being out of the sun. There was a smell of dust in the air, the acrid mixed odour of the destroyed ceiling board and the creosote-impregnated timbers that had repelled the ants.

Mma Potsane gestured about the room in which they were standing. "You see. There is nothing here. It is just an empty house. We can leave now."

Mma Ramotswe ignored the suggestion. She was studying a piece of yellowing paper which had been pinned to a wall. It was newspaper photograph – a picture of a man standing in front of a building. There had been a printed caption, but the paper had rotted and it was illegible. She beckoned for Mma Potsane to join her.

"Who is this man?

Mma Potsane peered at the photograph, holding it close to her eyes. "I remember that man," she said. "He worked here too. He is a Motswana. He was very friendly with the American. They used to spend all their time talking, talking, like two old men at a *kgotla*."

"Was he from the village?" asked Mma Ramotswe.

Mma Potsane laughed. "No, he wasn't one of us. He was from Francistown. His father was headmaster there and he was a very clever man. This one too, the son; he was very clever. He knew many things. That was why the American was always talking to him. The German didn't like him, though. Those two were not friends."

Mma Ramotswe studied the photograph, and then gently took it off the wall and tucked it into her pocket. Mma Potsane had moved away, and she joined her, peering into the next room. Here, on the floor, there lay the skeleton of a large bird, trapped in the house and unable to get out. The bones lay where the bird must have fallen, picked clean by ants.

"This was the room they used as an office," said Mma Potsane. "They kept all the receipts and they had a small safe over there, in that corner. People sent them money, you know. There were people in other countries who thought that this place was important. They believed that it could show that dry places like this could be changed. They wanted us to show that people could live together in a place like this and share everything."

Mma Ramotswe nodded. She was familiar with people who liked to test out all sorts of theories about how people might live. There was something about the country that attracted them, as if in that vast, dry country there was enough *air* for new ideas to breathe. Such people had been excited when the Brigade movement had been set up. They had thought it a very good idea that young people should be asked to spend time working for others and helping to build their country; but what was so exceptional about that? Did young people not work in rich countries? Perhaps they did not, and that is why these people, who came from such countries, should have found the whole idea so exciting. There was nothing wrong with these people – they were kind people usually, and treated the Batswana with respect. Yet somehow it could be *tiring* to be given advice. There was always some eager foreign organisation ready to say to Africans:

[83]

this is what you do, this is how you should do things. The advice may be good, and it might work elsewhere, but Africa needed its own solutions.

This farm was yet another example of one of these schemes that did not work out. You could not grow vegetables in the Kalahari. That was all there was to it. There were many things that could grow in a place like this, but these were things that belonged here. They were not like tomatoes and lettuces. They did not belong in Botswana, or at least not in this part of it.

They left the office and wandered through the rest of the house. Several of the rooms were open to the sky, and the floors in these rooms were covered in leaves and twigs. Lizards darted for cover, rustling the leaves, and tiny, pink and white geckoes froze where they clung to the walls, taken aback by the totally unfamiliar intrusion. Lizards; geckoes; the dust in the air; this was all it was – an empty house.

Save for the photograph.

Mma Potsane was pleased once they were out again, and suggested that she show Mma Ramotswe the place where the vegetables had been grown. Again, the land had reasserted itself, and all that remained to show of the scheme was a pattern of wandering ditches, now eroded into tiny canyons. Here and there, it was possible to see where the wooden poles supporting the shade–netting had been erected, but there was no trace of the wood itself, which, like everything else, had been consumed by the ants.

Mma Ramotswe shaded her eyes with a hand.

"All that work," she mused. "And now this."

Mma Potsane shrugged her shoulders. "But that is always true, Mma," she said. "Even Gaborone. Look at all those buildings. How do we know that Gaborone will still be there in fifty years' time? Have the ants not got their plans for

Gaborone as well?"

Mma Ramotswe smiled. It was a good way of putting it. All our human endeavours are like that, she reflected, and it is only because we are too ignorant to realize it, or are too forgetful to remember it, that we have the confidence to build something that is meant to last. Would the No. 1 Ladies' Detective Agency be remembered in twenty years time? Or Tlokweng Road Speedy Motors? Probably not, but then did it matter all that much?

The melancholy thought prompted her to remember. She was not here to dream about archaeology but to try to find out something about what happened all those years ago. She had come to read a place, and had found that there was nothing, or almost nothing, to be read. It was as if the wind had come and rubbed it all out, scattering the pages, covering the footsteps with dust.

She turned to Mma Potsane, who was silent beside her.

"Where does the wind come from, Mma Potsane?"

The other woman touched her cheek, in a gesture which Mma Ramotswe did not understand. Her eyes looked empty, Mma Ramotswe thought; one had dulled, and was slightly milky; she should go to a clinic.

"Over there," said Mma Potsane, pointing out to the thorn trees and the long expanse of sky, to the Kalahari. "Over there."

Mma Ramotswe said nothing. She was very close, she felt, to understanding what had happened, but she could not express it, and she could not tell why she knew.

CHAPTER TEN

Children are good for Botswana

M R J.L.B. MATEKONI'S BAD-TEMPERED maid was slouching at the kitchen door, her battered red hat at a careless, angry angle. Her mood had become worse since her employer had revealed his unsettling news, and her waking hours had been spent in contemplating how she might avert catastrophe. The arrangement which she had with Mr J.L.B. Matekoni suited her very well. There was not a great deal of work to do; men never worried about cleaning and polishing, and provided they were well fed they were very untroublesome employers. And she did feed Mr J.L.B. Matekoni well, no matter what that fat woman might be saying to the contrary. She had said that he was too thin! Thin by her standards perhaps, but quite well built by the standards of any normal people. She could just imagine what she had in store for him – spoonfuls of lard for breakfast and thick slices of bread, which would puff him up like that fat chief from the north, the one who broke the chair when he went to visit the house where her cousin worked as a maid.

But it was not so much the welfare of Mr J.L.B. Matekoni that concerned her, it was her own threatened position. If she had to go off and work in a hotel she would not be able to entertain her men friends in that same way. Under the current arrangement, men were able to visit her in the house while her employer was at work – without his knowledge, of course – and they were able to go into Mr J.L.B. Matekoni's room where there was the large double bed which he had bought from Central Furnishers. It was very comfortable – wasted on a bachelor, really – and the men liked it. They gave her presents of money, and the gifts were always better if they were able to spend time together in Mr J.L.B. Matekoni's room. That would all come to an end if anything changed.

The maid frowned. The situation was serious enough to merit desperate action, but it was hard to see what she could do. There was no point trying to reason with him; once a woman like that had sunk her claws into a man then there would be no turning him back. Men became quite unreasonable in such circumstances and he simply would not listen to her if she tried to tell him of the dangers that lay ahead. Even if she found out something about that woman – something about her past – he would probably pay no attention to the disclosure. She imagined confronting Mr J.L.B. Matekoni with the information that his future wife was a murderess! That woman has already killed two husbands, she might say. She put something in their food. They are both dead now because of her.

But he would say nothing, and just smile. I do not believe you, he would retort; and he would continue to say that even if she waved the headlines from the *Botswana Daily News*: *Mma Ramotswe murders husband with poison. Police take porridge away and do tests. Porridge found to be full of poison.* No, he would not believe it.

She spat into the dust. If there was nothing that she could do to get him to change his mind, then perhaps she had better think about doing some way of dealing with Mma Ramotswe. If Mma Ramotswe were simply not there, then the problem would have been solved. If she could ... No, it was a terrible thing to think, and then she probably would not be able to afford to hire a witchdoctor. They were very expensive when it came to removing people, and it was far too risky anyway. People talked, and the police would come round, and she could imagine nothing worse than going to

[87]

prison.

Prison! What if Mma Ramotswe were to be sent to prison for a few years? You can't marry somebody who is in prison, and they can't marry you. So if Mma Ramotswe were to be found to have committed a crime and be sent off for a few years, then all would stay exactly as it was. And did it really matter if she had not actually committed a crime, as long as the police thought that she had and they were able to find the evidence? She had heard once of how a man had been sent off to prison because his enemies had planted ammunition in his house and had informed the police that he was storing it for guerillas. That was back in the days of the Zimbabwe war, when Mr Nkomo had his men near Francistown and bullets and guns were coming into the country no matter how hard the police tried to stop them. The man had protested his innocence, but the police had just laughed, and the magistrate had laughed too.

There were few bullets and guns these days, but it might still be possible to find something that could be hidden in her house. What did the police look for these days? They were very worried about drugs, she believed, and the newspapers sometimes wrote about this person or that person being arrested for trading in *dagga*. But they had to have a large amount before the police were interested and where would she be able to lay her hands on that? *Dagga* was expensive and she could probably afford no more than a few leaves. So it would have to be something else.

The maid thought. A fly had landed on her forehead and was crawling down the ridge of her nose. Normally she would have brushed it away, but a thought had crossed her mind and it was developing deliciously. The fly was ignored: a dog barked in the neighbouring garden; a truck changed gear noisily on the road to the old airstrip. The maid smiled, and pushed her hat back. One of her men friends could help her.

She knew what he did, and she knew that it was dangerous. He could deal with Mma Ramotswe, and in return she would give him those attentions which he so clearly enjoyed but which were denied him at home. Everybody would be happy. He would get what he wanted. She would save her job. Mr J.L.B.Matekoni would be saved from a predatory woman, and Mma Ramotswe would get her just deserts. It was all very clear.

The maid returned to the kitchen and started to peel some potatoes. Now that the threat posed by Mma Ramotswe was receding – or shortly would – she felt quite positively disposed towards her wayward employer, who was just weak, like all men. She would cook him a fine lunch today. There was meat in the fridge – meat which she had earlier planned to take home with her, but which she would now fry up for him with a couple of onions and a good helping of mashed potatoes.

The meal was not quite ready when Mr J.L.B. Matekoni came home. She heard his truck and the sound of the gate slamming, and then the door opening. He usually called out when he came back - a simple "I'm home now" to let her know that she could put his lunch on the table. Today, though, there was no shout; instead, there was the sound of another voice. She caught her breath. The thought occurred to her that he might have come home with that woman, having asked her to lunch. In that case, she would hurriedly hide the stew and say that there was no food in the house. She could not bear the thought of Mma Ramotswe eating her food; she would rather feed it to a dog than lay it before the woman who had threatened her livelihood.

She moved towards the kitchen door and peered down the corridor. Just inside the front door, holding it open to let somebody follow him into the house, was Mr J.L.B. Matekoni.

"Careful," he said. "This door is not very wide."

Another voice answered, but she did not hear what it said. It was a female voice but not, she realised with a rush of relief, the voice of that terrible woman. Who was he bringing back to the house? Another woman? That would be good, because then she could tell that Ramotswe woman that he was not faithful to her and that might put an end to the marriage before it started.

But then the wheelchair came in and she saw the girl, pushed by her small brother, enter the house. She was at a loss what to think. What was her employer doing bringing these children into the house? They must be relatives; the children of some distant cousin. The old Botswana morality dictated that you had to provide for such people, no matter how distant the connection.

"I am here, Rra," she called out. "Your lunch is ready."

Mr J.L.B. Matekoni looked up. "Ah," he said. "There are some children with me. They will need to eat."

"There will be enough,"she called out. "I have made a good stew."

She waited a few minutes before going into the living room, busying herself with the mashing of the over-cooked potatoes. When she did go through, wiping her hands industriously on a kitchen rag, she found Mr J.L.B. Matekoni sitting in his chair. On the other side of the room, looking out of the window, was a girl, with a young boy, presumably her brother, standing beside her. The maid stared at the children, taking in at a glance what sort of children they were. Basarwa, she thought: unmistakeable. The girl had that colour skin, the light brown, the colour of cattle dung; the boy had those eyes that those people have, a bit like Chinese eyes, and his buttocks stuck out in a little shelf behind him.

"These children have come to live here," said Mr J.L.B.

[90]

Matekoni, lowering his eyes as he spoke. "They are from the orphan farm, but I am going to be looking after them."

The maid's eyes widened. She had not expected this. Masarwa children being brought into an ordinary person's house and allowed to live there was something no self-respecting person would do. These people were thieves – she never doubted that – and they should not be encouraged to come and live in respectable Batswana houses. Mr J.L.B. Matekoni may be trying to be kind, but there were limits to charity.

She stared at her employer. "They are staying here? For how many days?"

He did not look up at her. He was too ashamed, she thought.

"They are staying here for a long time. I am not planning to take them back."

She was silent. She wondered whether this had something to do with that Ramotswe woman. She might have decided that the children could come and stay as part of her programme to take over his life. First you move in some Masarwa children, and then you move in yourself. The moving in of the children may even have been part of a plot against herself, of course. Mma Ramotswe might well have expected that she would not approve of such children coming into the house and in this way she might force her out even before she moved in altogether. Well, if that was her plan, then she would do everything in her power to thwart it. She would show her that she liked these children and that she was happy to have them in the house. It would be difficult, but she could do it.

"You will be hungry," she said to the girl, smiling as she spoke. "I have some good stew. It is just what children like."

The girl returned the smile. "Thank you, Mma," she said respectfully. "You are very kind."

The boy said nothing. He was looking at the maid with

[91]

those disconcerting eyes, and it made her shudder inwardly. She returned to the kitchen and prepared the plates. She gave the girl a good helping, and there was plenty for Mr J.L.B. Matekoni. But to the boy she gave only a small amount of stew, and covered most of that with the scrapings from the potato pot. She did not want to encourage that child, and the less he had to eat the better.

The meal was taken in silence. Mr J.L.B. Matekoni sat at the head of the table, with the girl at his right and the boy at the other end. The girl had to lean forward in her chair to eat, as the table was so constructed that the wheelchair would not fit underneath it. But she managed well enough, and soon finished her helping. The boy wolfed down his food and then sat with his hands politely clasped together, watching Mr J.L.B. Matekoni.

Afterwards, Mr J.L.B. Matekoni went out to the truck and fetched the suitcase which they have brought from the orphan farm. The housemother had issued them with extra clothes and these had been placed in one of the cheap brown cardboard suitcases which the orphans were given when they went out into the world. There was small, typed list taped to the top of the case, and this listed the clothes issued under two columns. *Boy: 2 pairs boy's pants, 2 pairs khaki shorts, 2 khaki shirts, 1 jersey, 4 socks, 1 pair shoes, 1 Setswana Bible. Girl: 3 pairs girl's pants, 2 shirts, 1 vest, 2 skirts, 4 socks, 1 pair shoes, 1 Setswana Bible.*

He took the suitcase inside and showed the children to the room they were to occupy, the small room he had kept for the visitors who never seemed to arrive, the room with two mattresses, a small pile of dusty blankets, and a chair. He placed the suitcase on the chair and opened it. The girl wheeled herself over to the chair and looked in at the clothes, which were new. She reached forward and touched them hesitantly, lovingly, as one would who had never before possessed new clothes.

Mr J.L.B. Matekoni left them to unpack. Going out into the garden, he stood for a moment under his shade-netting by the front door. He knew that he had done something momentous in bringing the children to the house, and now the full immensity of his action came home to him. He had changed the course of the lives of two other people and now everything that happened to them would be his responsibility. For a moment he felt appalled by the thought. Not only were there were two extra mouths to feed, but there were schools to thinks about, and a woman to look after their day-to-day needs. He would have to find a nursemaid – a man could never do all the things that children need to have done for them. Some sort of housemother, rather like the housemother who had looked after them at the orphan farm. He stopped. He had forgotten. He was almost a married man. Mma Ramotswe would be mother to these children.

He sat down heavily on an upturned petrol drum. These children were Mma Ramotswe's responsibility now, and he had not even asked her opinion. He had allowed himself to be bamboozled into taking them by that persuasive Mma Potokwane, and he had hardly thought out all the implications. Could he take them back? She could hardly refuse to receive them as they were still, presumably, her legal responsibility. Nothing had been signed; there were no pieces of paper which could be waved in his face. But to take them back was unthinkable. He had told the children that he would look after them, and that, in his mind, was more important than any signature on a legal document.

Mr J.L.B. Matekoni had never broken his word. He had made it a rule of his business life that he would never tell a customer something and then not stick to what he had said. Sometimes this had cost him dearly. If he told a customer that a repair to a car would cost three hundred pula, then he would never charge more than that, even if he discovered that the work took far longer. And often it did take longer, with those lazy apprentices of his taking hours to do even the simplest thing. He could not understand how it would be possible to take three hours to do a simple service on a car. All you had to do was to drain the old oil and pour it into the dirty oil container. Then you put in fresh oil, changed the oil filters, checked the brake fluid level, adjusted the timing, and greased the gearbox. That was the simple service, which cost two hundred and eighty pula. It could be done in an hour and a half at the most, but the apprentices managed to take much longer.

No, he could not go back on the assurance he had given those children. They were his children, come what may. He would talk to Mma Ramotswe and explain to her that children were good for Botswana and that they should do what they could to help these poor children who had no people of their own. She was a good woman, he knew, and he was sure that she would understand and agree with him. Yes, he would do it, but perhaps not just yet.

CHAPTER ELEVEN

The Glass Ceiling

M MA MAKUTSI, SECRETARY of the No. 1 Ladies' Detective
Agency and *cum laude* graduate of the Botswana Secretarial College, sat at her desk, staring out through the open
door. She preferred to leave the door open when there was
nothing happening in the agency (which was most of the time),
but it had its drawbacks, as the chickens would sometimes
wander in and strut about as if they were in a henhouse. She
did not like these chickens, for a number of very sound reasons. To begin with, there was something unprofessional
about having chickens in a detective agency, and then, quite
apart from that, the chickens themselves irritated her profoundly. It was always the same group of chickens: four hens
and a dispirited and, she imagined, impotent rooster, who
was kept on by the hens out of charity. The rooster was lame
and had lost a large proportion of the feathers on one of his
wings. He looked defeated, as if he were only too well aware
of his loss of status, and he always walked several steps behind the hens themselves, like a royal consort relegated by
protocol into a permanent second place.

The hens seemed equally irritated by Mma Makutsi's presence. It was as if she, rather than they, were the intruder. By
rights, this tiny building with its two small windows and its
creaky door should be a henhouse, not a detective agency. If
they outstared her, perhaps, she would go, and they would
be left to perch on the chairs and make their nests in the
filing cabinets. That is what the chickens wanted.

"Get out," said Mma Makutsi, waving a folded-up newspaper at them. "No chickens here! Get out!"

The largest of the hens turned and glared at her, while the rooster merely looked shifty.

"I mean you!" shouted Mma Makutsi. "This is not a chicken farm. Out!"

The hens uttered an indignant clucking and seemed to hesitate for a moment. But when Mma Makutsi pushed her chair back and made to get up, they turned and began to move towards the door, the rooster in the lead this time, limping awkwardly.

The chickens dealt with, Mma Makutsi resumed her staring out of the door. She resented the indignity of having to shoo chickens out of one's office. How many first-class graduates of the Botswana Secretarial College had to do that, she wondered. There were offices in town – large buildings with wide windows and air-conditioning units where the secretaries sat at polished desks with chrome handles. She had seen these offices when the college had taken them for work-experience visits. She had seen them sitting there, smiling, wearing expensive ear-rings and waiting for a well-paid husband to step forward and ask them to marry him. She had thought at the time that she would like a job like that, although she herself would be more interested in the work than in the husband. She had assumed, in fact, that such a job would be hers, but when the course had finished and they had all gone off for interviews, she had received no offers. She could not understand why this should be so. Some of the other women who got very much worse marks than she did – sometimes as low as 51 per cent (the barest of passes) received good offers whereas she (who had achieved the almost inconceivable mark of 97 per cent) received nothing. How could this be?

It was one of the other unsuccessful girls who explained it to her. She, too, had gone to interviews and been unlucky.

"It is men who give out these jobs, am I right?" she had said.

"I suppose so," said Mma Makutsi. "Men run these businesses. They choose the secretaries."

"So how do you think men choose who should get the job and who shouldn't? Do you think they choose by the marks we got? Is that how you think they do it?"

Mma Makutsi was silent. It had never occurred to her that decisions of this nature would be made on any other basis. Everything that she had been taught at school had conveyed the message that hard work helped you to get a good job.

"Well," said her friend, smiling wryly, "I can tell that you do think that. And you're wrong. Men choose women for jobs on the basis of their looks. They choose the beautiful ones and give them jobs. To the others, they say: We are very sorry. All the jobs have gone. We are very sorry. There is a world recession, and in a world recession there are only enough jobs for beautiful girls. That is the effect of a world recession. It is all economics."

Mma Makutsi had listened in astonishment. But she knew, even as the bitter remarks were uttered, that they were true. Perhaps she had known all along, at a subconscious level, and had simply not faced up the fact. Good-looking women got what they wanted and women like her, who was perhaps not so elegant as the others, were left with nothing.

That evening she looked in the mirror. She had tried to do something about her hair, but had failed. She had applied hair-straightener and had pulled and tugged at it, but it had remained completely uncooperative. And her skin, too, had resisted the creams that she had applied to it, with the result that her complexion was far darker than that of almost very other girl at the college. She felt a flush of resentment at her fate. It was hopeless. Even with those large round glasses she had bought herself, at such crippling expense, could not disguise the fact that she was a dark girl in a world where light-coloured girls with heavily applied red lipstick had everything at their disposal. That was the ultimate, inescapable truth that no amount of wishful thinking, no amount of expensive creams and lotions, could change. The fun in this life, the good jobs, the rich husbands, were not a matter of merit and hard work, but were a matter of brute, unshifting biology.

Mma Makutsi stood before the mirror and cried. She had worked and worked for her 97 per cent at the Botswana Secretarial College, but she might as well have spent her time having fun and going out with boys, for all the good that it had done her. Would there be a job at all, or would she stay at home helping her mother to wash and iron her younger brothers' khaki pants?

The question was answered the next day when she applied for and was given the job of Mma Ramotswe's secretary. Here was the solution. If men refused to appoint on merit, then go for a job with a woman. It may not be a glamorous office, but it was certainly an exciting thing to be. To be secretary to a private detective was infinitely more prestigious than to be a secretary in a bank or in a lawyer's office. So perhaps there was some justice after all. Perhaps all that work had been worthwhile after all.

But there was still this problem with the chickens.

"So, Mma Makutsi," said Mma Ramotswe, as she settled herself down in her chair in anticipation of the pot of bush tea which her secretary was brewing for her. "So I went off to Molepolole and found the place where those people lived. I saw the farmhouse and the place where they tried to grow the vegetables. I spoke to a woman who had lived there at the time. I saw everything there was to see."

"And you found something?" asked Mma Makutsi, as she poured the hot water into the old enamel teapot and swirled it around with the tea leaves.

"I found a feeling," said Mma Ramotswe. "I felt that I knew something."

Mma Makutsi listened to her employer. What did she mean by saying that she felt she knew something. Either you know something or you don't. You can't think that you might know something, if you didn't actually know what it was that you were meant to know.

"I am not sure ..." she began.

Mma Ramotswe laughed. "It's called an intuition. You can read about it in Mr Andersen's book. He talks about intuitions. They tell us things that we know deep inside, but which we can't find the word for."

"And this intuition you felt at that place," said Mma Makutsi hesitantly. "What did it tell you? Where this poor American boy was?"

"There," said Mma Ramotswe quietly. "That young man is there."

For a moment they were both silent. Mma Makutsi lowered the teapot on to the formica table-top and replaced the lid.

"He is living out there? Still?"

"No," said Mma Ramotswe. "He is dead. But he is there. Do you know what I am talking about?"

Mma Makutsi nodded. She knew. Any sensitive person in Africa would know what Mma Ramotswe meant. When we die, we do not leave the place we were in when we were alive. We are still there, in a sense; our spirit is there. It never goes away. This was something which white people simply did not understand. They called it superstition, and said that it was a sign of ignorance to believe in such things. But they were the ones who were ignorant. If they could not understand how we are part of the natural world about us, then they are the ones who have closed eyes, not us.

Mma Makutsi poured the tea and handed Mma Ramotswe her mug.

"Are you going to tell the American woman this?" she asked. "Surely she will say: 'Where is the body? Show me the exact place where my son is.' You know how these people think. She will not understand you if you say that he is there somewhere, but you cannot point to the spot."

Mma Ramotswe raised the mug to her lips, watching her secretary as she spoke. This was an astute woman, she thought. She understood exactly how the American woman would think, and she appreciated just how difficult it could be to convey these subtle truths to one who conceived of the world as being entirely explicable by science. The Americans were very clever; they sent rockets into space and invented machines which could think more quickly than any human being alive, but all this cleverness could also make them blind. They did not understand other people. They thought that everyone looked at things in the same way as Americans did, but they were wrong. Science was only part of the truth. There were also many other things that made the world what it was, and the Americans often failed to notice these things, although they were there all the time, under their noses.

Mma Ramotswe put down her mug of tea and reached into the pocket of her dress.

"I also found this," she said, extracting the folded newspaper photograph and passing it to her secretary. Mma Makutsi unfolded the piece of paper and smoothed it out on the surface of her desk. She gazed at it for a few moments before looking up at Mma Ramotswe.

"This is very old," she said. "Was it lying there?"

"No. It was on the wall. There were still some papers pinned on a wall. The ants had missed them."

Mma Makutsi returned her gaze to the paper.

"There are names," she said. "Cephas Kalumani. Oswald Ranta. Mma Soloi. Who are these people?"

"They lived there," said Mma Ramotswe. "They must have been there at the time."

Mma Makutsi shrugged her shoulders. "But even if we could find these people and talk to them," she said, "would that make any difference? The police must have talked to them at the time. Maybe even Mma Curtin talked to them herself when she first came back."

Mma Ramotswe nodded her head in agreement. "You're right," she said. "But that photograph tells me something. Look at the faces."

Mma Makutsi studied the yellowing image. There were two men in the front, standing next to a woman. Behind them was another man, his face indistinct, and a woman, whose back was half-turned. The names in the caption referred to the three in the front. Cephas Kalumani was a tall man, with slightly gangly limbs, a man who would look awkward and ill at ease in any photograph. Mma Soloi, who was standing next to him, was beaming with pleasure. She was a comfortable woman – the archetypical, hard-working Motswana woman, the sort of woman who supported a large family, whose life's labour, it seemed, would be devoted to endless, uncomplaining cleaning: cleaning the yard, cleaning the house, cleaning children. This was picture of a heroine; unacknowledged, but a heroine nonetheless.

The third figure, Oswald Ranta, was another matter altogether. He was a well-dressed, dapper figure. He was wearing a white shirt and tie and, like Mma Soloi, was smiling at the camera. His smile, though, was very different.

"Look at that man," said Mma Ramotswe. "Look at Ranta."

"I do not like him," said Mma Makutsi. "I do not like the

look of him at all."

"Precisely," said Mma Ramotswe. "That man is evil."

Mma Makutsi said nothing, and for a few minutes the two of them sat in total silence, Mma Makutsi staring at the photograph and Mma Ramotswe looking down into her mug of tea. Then Mma Ramotswe spoke.

"I think that if anything bad was done in that place, then it was done by that man. Do you think I am right?"

"Yes," said Mma Makutsi. "You are right." She paused. "Are you going to find him now?"

"That is my next task," said Mma Ramotswe. "I shall ask around and see if anybody knows this man. But in the meantime, we have some letters to write, Mma. We have other cases to think about. That man at the brewery who was anxious about his brother. I have found out something now and we can write to him. But first we must write a letter about that accountant."

Mma Makutsi inserted a piece of paper into her typewriter and waited for Mma Ramotswe to dictate. The letter was not an interesting one – it was all about the tracing of a company accountant who had sold most of the company's assets and then disappeared. The police had stopped looking for him but the company wanted to trace its property.

Mma Makutsi typed automatically. Her mind was not on the task, but her training enabled her to type accurately even if she was thinking about something else. Now she was thinking of Oswald Ranta, and of how they might trace him. The spelling of Ranta was slightly unusual, and the simplest thing would be to look the name up in the telephone directory. Oswald Ranta was a smart-looking man who could be expected to have a telephone. All she had to do was to look him up and write down the address. Then she could go and make her own enquiries, if she wished, and present Mma Ramotswe with the information.

The letter finished, she passed it over to Mma Ramotswe for signature and busied herself with addressing the envelope. Then, while Mma Ramotswe made a note in the file, she slipped open her drawer and took out the Botswana telephone directory. As she had thought, there was only one Oswald Ranta.

"I must make a quick telephone call," she said. "I shall only be a moment."

Mma Ramotswe grunted her assent. She knew that Mma Makutsi could be trusted with the telephone, unlike most secretaries, who she knew used their employers' telephones to make all sorts of long-distance calls to boyfriends in remote places like Maun or Orapa.

Mma Makutsi spoke in a low voice, and Mma Ramotswe did not hear her.

"Is Rra Ranta there, please?"

"He is at work, Mma. I am the maid."

"I'm sorry to bother you, Mma. I must phone him at work. Can you tell me where that is?"

"He is at the University. He goes there every day."

"I see. Which number there?"

She noted it down on a piece of paper, thanked the maid, and replaced the receiver. Then she dialled, and again her pencil scratched across paper.

"Mma Ramotswe," she said quietly. " I have all the information you need."

Mma Ramotswe looked up sharply.

"Information about what?"

"Oswald Ranta. He is living here in Gaborone. He is a lecturer in the Department of Rural Economics in the University. The secretary there says that he always comes in at eight o'clock every morning and that anybody who wishes to see him can make an appointment. You need not look any further."

Mma Ramotswe smiled.

"You are a very clever person," she said. "How did you find all this out?"

"I looked in the telephone directory," answered Mma Makutsi. "Then I telephoned to find out about the rest."

"I see," said Mma Ramotswe, still smiling. "That was very good detective work."

Mma Makutsi beamed at the praise. Detective work. She had done the job of a detective, although she was only a secretary.

"I am happy that you are pleased with my work," she said, after a moment. "I have wanted to be a detective. I'm happy being a secretary, but it is not the same thing as being a detective."

Mma Ramotswe frowned. "This is what you have wanted?"

"Every day," said Mma Makutsi. "Every day I have wanted this thing."

Mma Ramotswe thought about her secretary. She was a good worker, and intelligent, and if it meant so much to her, then why should she not be promoted? She could help her with her investigations, which would be a much better use of her time than sitting at her desk waiting for the telephone to ring. They could buy an answering machine to deal with calls if she was out of the office on an investigation. Why not give her the chance and make her happy?

"You shall have the thing you have wanted," said Mma Ramotswe. "You will be promoted to assistant detective. As from tomorrow."

Mma Makutsi rose to her feet. She opened her mouth to speak, but the emotion within her strangled any words. She sat down.

"I am glad that you are pleased," said Mma Ramotswe. "You have broken the glass ceiling that stops secretaries from reaching their full potential."

Mma Makutsi looked up, as if to search for the ceiling that she had broken. There were only the familiar ceiling boards, fly-tracked and buckling from the heat. But the ceiling of the Sistine Chapel itself could not at that moment have been more glorious in her eyes, more filled with hope and joy.

CHAPTER TWELVE

At Night in Gaborone

ALONE IN HER house in Zebra Drive, Mma Ramotswe awoke, as she often did, in the small hours of the morning, that time when the town was utterly silent; the time of maximum danger for rats, and other small creatures, as cobras and mambas moved silently in their hunting. She had always suffered from broken sleep, but had stopped worrying about it. She never lay awake for more than an hour or so, and, since she retired to bed early, she always managed at least seven hours of sleep a night. She had read that people needed eight hours, and that the body eventually claimed its due. If that were so, then she made up for it, as she often slept for several hours on a Saturday and never got up early on Sunday. So an hour or so lost at two or three each morning was nothing significant.

Recently, while waiting to have her hair braided at the Make Me Beautiful Salon she had noticed a magazine article on sleep. There was a famous doctor, she read, who knew all about sleep and had several words of advice for those whose sleep was troubled. This Dr Shapiro had a special clinic just for people who could not sleep and he attached wires to their heads to see what was wrong. Mma Ramotswe was intrigued: there was a picture of Dr Shapiro and a sleepy-looking man and woman, in dishevelled pyjamas, with a tangle of wires coming from their heads. She felt immediately sorry for them: the woman, in particular, looked miserable, like somebody who was being forced to participate in an immensely tedious procedure but who simply could not escape. Or was she miserable because of the hospital pyjamas, in which she was being photographed; she may always have wished to have her photograph in a magazine, and now her wish was to be fulfilled – in hospital pyjamas.

And then she read on, and became outraged. "Fat people often have difficulty in sleeping well," the article went on. "They suffer from a condition called sleep apnoea, which means that their breathing is interrupted in sleep. Such people are advised to lose weight."

Advised to lose weight! What has weight to do with it? There were many fat people who seemed to sleep perfectly well; indeed, there was a fat person who often sat under a tree outside Mma Ramotswe's house and who seemed to be asleep most of the time. Would one advise that person to lose weight? It seemed to Mma Ramotswe as if such advice would be totally unnecessary and would probably simply lead to unhappiness. From being a fat person who was comfortably placed in the shade of a tree, this poor person would become a thin person, with not much of a bottom to sit upon, and probably unable to sleep as a result.

And what about her own case? She was a fat lady – *traditionally built* – and yet she had no difficulty in getting the required amount of sleep. It was all part of this terrible *attack* on people by those who had nothing better to do than to give advice on all sorts of subjects. These people, who wrote in newspapers and talked on the radio, were full of good ideas as to how to make people better. They poked their noses into other people's affairs, telling them to do this and do that. They looked at what you were eating and told you it was bad for you; then they looked at the way you raised your children and said that was bad too. And to make matters worse, they often said that if you did not heed their warnings, you would die. In this way they made everybody so frightened of them that they felt they had to accept the advice.

There were two main targets, Mma Ramotswe thought. First, there were fat people, who were now getting quite used to a relentless campaign against them; and then there were men. Mma Ramotswe knew that men were far from perfect – that many men were very wicked and selfish and lazy, and that they had, by and large, made rather a bad job of running Africa. But that was no reason to treat them badly, as some of these people did. There were plenty of good men about – people like Mr J.L.B. Matekoni, Sir Sereste Khama (First President of Botswana, Statesman, Paramount Chief of the Bangwato), and the late Obed Ramotswe, retired miner, expert judge of cattle, and her much-loved daddy.

She missed the Daddy, and not a day went by, not one, that she did not think of him. Often when she awoke at this hour of the night, and lay alone in the darkness, she would search her memory to retrieve some recollection of him that had alluded her: some scrap of conversation, some gesture, some shared experience. Each memory was a precious treasure to her, fondly dwelt upon, sacramental in its significance. Obed Ramotswe, who had loved his daughter, and who had saved every rand, every cent, that he made in those cruel mines, and had built up that fine herd of cattle for her sake, had asked for nothing for himself. He did not drink, he did not smoke; he thought only of her and of what would happen to her.

If only she could erase those two awful years spent with Note Mokoti, when she knew that her daddy had suffered so much, knowing, as he did, that Note would only make her unhappy. When she had returned to him, after Note's departure, and he had seen, even as he had embraced her, the scar of the latest beating, he had said nothing, and had stopped her explanation in its tracks.

"You do not have to tell me about it," he said. "We do not have to talk about it. It is over."

She had wanted to say sorry to him – to say that she should have asked his opinion of Note before she had married him, and listened, but she felt too raw for this and he would not have wanted it.

And she remembered his illness, when his chest had become more and more congested with the disease which killed so many miners, and how she had held his hand at his bedside and how, afterwards, she had gone outside, dazed, wanting to wail, as would be proper, but silent in her grief; and how she had seen a Go-Away bird staring at her from the bough of a tree, and how it had fluttered up, on to a higher branch, and turned round to stare at her again, before flying off; and of a red car that at that moment had passed in the road, with two children in the back, dressed in white dresses, with ribbons in their hair, who had looked at her too, and had waved. And of how the sky looked – heavy with rain, purple clouds stacked high up one another, and of lightning in the distance, over the Kalahari, linking sky to earth. And of a woman who, not knowing that the world had just ended for her, called out to her from the verandah of the hospital: *Come inside, Mma. Do not stand there! There is going to be a storm. Come inside quickly!*

Not far away, a small plane on its way to Gaborone flew low over the dam and then, losing height, floated down over the area known as the Village, over the cluster of shops on the Tlokweng Road, and finally, in the last minute of its journey, over the houses that dotted the bush on the airstrip boundary. In one of these, at a window, a girl sat watching. She had been up for an hour or so, as her sleep had been disturbed, and she had decided to get up from her bed and look out of the window. The wheelchair was beside the bed and she was able to manoeuvre herself into it without help. Then, propelling herself over to the open window, she had sat and looked out into the night.

She had heard the plane before she saw its lights. She had wondered what a plane was doing coming in at three in the morning. How could pilots fly at night? How could they tell where they were going in that limitless darkness? What if they took a wrong turning and went out over the Kalahari, where there were no lights to guide them and where it would be like flying within a dark cave?

She watched the plane fly almost directly above the house, and saw the shape of the wings and the cone of brightness which the landing light of the plane projected before it. The noise of the engine was loud now – not just a distant buzz – but a heavy, churning sound. Surely it would wake the household, she thought, but when the plane had dropped down on to the airstrip and the engine faded, the house was still in silence.

The girl looked out. There was a light off in the distance somewhere, maybe at the airstrip itself, but apart from that there was only darkness. The house looked away from the town, not towards it, and beyond the edge of the garden there was only scrub bush, trees and clumps of grass, and thorn bushes, and the odd red mud outcrop of a termite mound.

She felt alone. There were two other sleepers in that house: her younger brother, who never woke up at night, and the kind man who had fixed her wheelchair and who had then taken them in. She was not frightened to be here; she trusted that man to look after them – he was like Mr Jameson, who was the director of the charity that ran the orphan farm. He was a good man, who thought only about the orphans and their needs. At first, she had been unable to understand how there should be people like that. Why did people care for others, who were not even their family? She looked after her brother, but that was her duty.

The housemother had tried to explain it to her one day.

"We must look after other people," she had said. "Other people are our brothers and sisters. If they are unhappy, then we are unhappy. If they are hungry, then we are hungry. You see."

The girl had accepted this. It would be her duty, too, to look after other people. Even if she could never have a child herself, she would look after other children. And she could try to look after this kind man, Mr J.L.B. Matekoni, and make sure that everything in his house was clean and tidy. That would be her job.

There were some people who had mothers to look after them. She was not one of those people, she knew. But why had her mother died? She remembered her only vaguely now. She remembered her death, and the wailing from the other women. She remembered the baby being taken from her arms and put in the ground. She had dug him out, she believed, but was not sure. Perhaps somebody else had done that and had passed the boy on to her. And then she remembered going away and finding herself in a strange place.

Perhaps one day she would find a place where she would stay. That would be good. To know that the place you were in was your own place – where you should be.

CHAPTER FOURTEEN

A Problem in Moral Philosophy

THERE WERE SOME clients who engaged Mma Ramotswe's sympathies on the first telling of their tale. Others one could not sympathise with because they were motivated by selfishness, or greed, or sometimes self-evident paranoia. But the genuine cases – the cases which made the trade of private detective into a real calling – could break the heart. Mma Ramotswe knew that Mr Letsenyane Badule was one of these.

He came without an appointment, arriving the day after Mma Ramotswe had returned from her trip to Molepolole. It was the first day of Mma Makutsi's promotion to assistant detective, and Mma Ramotswe had just explained to her that although she was now a private detective she still had secretarial duties.

She had realised that she would have to broach the subject early, to avoid misunderstandings.

"I can't employ both a secretary and an assistant," she said. "This is a small agency. I do not make a big profit. You know that. You send out the bills."

Mma Makutsi's face had fallen. She was dressed in her smartest dress, and she had done something to her hair, which was standing on end in little pointed bunches. It had not worked.

"Am I still a secretary, then?" she said. "Do I still just do the typing?"

Mma Ramotswe shook her head. "I have not changed my mind," she said. "You are an assistant private detective. But somebody has to do the typing, don't they? That is a job for an assistant private detective. That, and other things."

Mma Makutsi's face brightened. "That is all right. I can do all the things I used to do, but I will do more as well. I shall have clients."

Mma Ramotswe drew in her breath. She had not envisaged giving Mma Makutsi her own clients. Her idea had been to assign her tasks to be performed under supervision. The actual management of cases was to be her own responsibility. But then she remembered. She remembered how, as girl she had worked in the Small Upright General Dealer Store in Mochudi and how thrilled she had been when she had first been allowed to do a stock-taking on her own. It was selfishness to keep the clients to herself. How could anybody be started on a career if those who were at the top kept all the interesting work for themselves?

"Yes," she said quietly. "You can have your own clients. But I will decide which ones you get. You may not get the very big clients ... to begin with. You can start with small matters and work up."

"That is quite fair," said Mma Makutsi. "Thank you, Mma. I do not want to run before I can walk. They told us that at the Botswana Secretarial College. Learn the easy things first and then learn the difficult things. Not the other way round."

"That's a good philosophy," said Mma Ramotswe. "Many young people these days have not been taught that. They want the big jobs right away. They want to start at the top, with lots of money and a big Mercedes Benz."

"That is not wise,' said Mma Makutsi. "Do the little things when you are young and then work up to doing the big things later."

"Mmm," mused Mma Ramotswe. "These Mercedes Benz cars have not been a good thing for Africa. They are very fine cars, I believe, but all the ambitious people in Africa want one before they have earned it. That has made for big problems."

"The more Mercedes Benzes there are in a country," offered Mma Makutsi, "the worse that country is. If there is a country without any Mercedes Benzes, then that will be a good place. You can count on that."

Mma Ramotswe stared at her assistant. It was an interesting theory, which could be discussed at greater length later on. For the meantime, there were one or two matters which still needed to be resolved.

"You will still make the tea," she said firmly. "You have always done that very well."

"I am very happy to do that," said Mma Makutsi, smiling. "There is no reason why an assistant private detective cannot make tea when there is nobody more junior to do it."

It had been an awkward discussion and Mma Ramotswe was pleased that it was over. She thought that it would be best if she gave her new assistant a case as soon as possible, to avoid the build-up of tension, and when, later that morning, Mr Letsenyane Badule arrived she decided that this would be a case for Mma Makutsi.

He drove up in a Mercedes Benz, but it was an old one, and therefore morally insignificant, with signs of rust around the rear sills and with a deep dent on the driver's door.

"I am not one who usually comes to private detectives," he said, sitting nervously on the edge of the comfortable chair reserved for clients. Opposite him, the two women smiled reassuringly. The fat woman – she was the boss, he knew, as he had seen her photograph in the newspaper – and that other one with the odd hair and the fancy dress, her assistant perhaps.

"You need not feel embarrassed," said Mma Ramotswe. "We have all sorts of people coming through this door. There is no shame in asking for help."

"In fact," interjected Mma Makutsi. "It is the strong ones who ask for help. It is the weak ones who are too ashamed to come."

Mma Ramotswe nodded. The client seemed to be reassured by what Mma Makutsi had said. This was a good sign. Not everyone knows how to set a client at ease, and it boded well that Mma Makutsi had shown herself able to chose her words well.

The tightness of Mr Badule's grip on the brim of his hat loosened, and he sat back in his chair.

"I have been very worried," he said. "Every night I have been waking up in the quiet hours and have been unable to get back to sleep. I lie in my bed and I turn this way and that and cannot get this one thought out of my head. All the time it is there, going round and round. Just one question, which I ask myself time after time after time."

"And you never find an answer?" said Mma Makutsi. "The night is a very bad times for questions to which there are no answers."

Mr Badule looked at her. "You are very right, my sister. There is nothing worse than a night-time question."

He stopped, and for a moment or two nobody spoke. Then Mma Ramotswe broke the silence.

"Why don't you tell us about yourself, Rra? Then a little bit later on, we can get to this question that is troubling you so badly. My assistant will make us a cup of tea first, and then we can drink it together."

Mr Badule nodded eagerly. He seemed close to tears for reason, and Mma Ramotswe knew that the ritual of tea, with the mugs hot against the hand, would somehow make the story flow and would ease the mind of this troubled man.

I am not a big, important man, began Mr Badule. I come from Lobatse originally. My father was an orderly at the High

[115]

Court there and he served many years. He worked for the British, and they gave him two medals, with the picture of the Queen's head on them. He wore these every day, even after he retired. When he left the service, one of the judges gave him a hoe to use on his lands. The judge had ordered the hoe to be made in the prison workshop and the prisoners, on the judge's instructions, had burned an inscription into the wooden handle with a hot nail. It said: *First Class Orderly Badule, served Her Majesty and then the Republic of Botswana loyally for fifty years. Well done tried and trusty servant, from Mr Justice Maclean, Puisne Judge, High Court of Botswana.*

That judge was a good man, and he was kind to me too. He spoke to one of the fathers at the Catholic School and they gave me a place in standard four. I worked hard at this school, and when I reported one of the other boys for stealing meat from the kitchen, they made me deputy-head boy.

I passed my Cambridge School certificate and afterwards I got a good job with the Meat Commission. I worked hard there too and again I reported other employees for stealing meat. I did not do this because I wanted promotion, but because I am not one who likes to see dishonesty in any form. That is one thing I learned from my father. As an orderly in the High Court, he saw all sorts of bad people, including murderers. He saw them standing in the court and telling lies because they knew that their wicked deeds had caught up with them. He watched them when the judges sentenced them to death and saw how big strong men who had beaten and stabbed other people became like little boys, terrified and sobbing and saying that they were sorry for all their bad deeds, which they had said they hadn't done anyway.

With such a background, it is not surprising that my father should have taught his sons to be honest and to tell the truth always. So I did not hesitate to bring these dishonest employees to justice and my employers were very pleased.

"You have stopped these wicked people from stealing the meat of Botswana," they said. "Our eyes cannot see what our employees are doing. Your eyes have helped us."

I did not expect a reward, but I was promoted. And in my new job, which was in the headquarters office, I found more people who were stealing meat, this time in a more indirect and clever way, but it was still stealing meat. So I wrote a letter to the General Manager and said: "Here is how you are losing meat, right under your noses, in the general office." And at the end I put the names, all in alphabetical order, and signed the letter and sent it off.

They were very pleased, and, as a result, they promoted me even further. By now, anybody who was dishonest had been frightened into leaving the company, and so there was no more work of that sort for me to do. But I still did well, and eventually I had saved enough money to buy my own butchery. I received a large cheque from the company, which was sorry to see me go, and I set up my butchery just outside Gaborone. You may have seen it on the road to Lobatse. It is called Honest Deal Butchery.

My butchery does quite well, but I do not have a lot of money to spare. The reason for this is my wife. She is a fashionable lady, who likes smart clothes and who does not like to work too much herself. I do not mind her not working, but it upsets me to see her spend so much money on braiding her hair and having new dresses made by the Indian tailor. I am not a smart man, but she is a very smart lady.

For many years after we got married there were no children. But then she became pregnant and we had a son. I was very proud, and my only sadness was that my father was not still alive so that he could see his fine new grandson.

My son is not very clever. We sent him to the primary school near our house and we keep getting reports saying that he had to try harder and that his handwriting was very untidy and full of mistakes. My wife said that he would have to be sent to a private school, where they would have better teachers and where they would force him to write more neatly, but I was worried that we could not afford that.

When I said that, she became very cross. "If you cannot pay for it," she said, "then I will go to a charity I know and get them to pay the fees."

"There are no such charities," I said. "If there were, then they would be inundated. Everyone wants his child to go t a private school. They would have every parent in Botswana lining up for help. It is impossible."

"Oh it is, is it?" she said. "I shall speak to this charity tomorrow, and you will see. You just wait and see."

She went off to town the next day and when she came back she said it had all been arranged. "The charity will pay all his school fees to go to Thornhill. He can start next term."

I was astonished. Thornhill, as you know, *Bomma*, is a very good school and the thought of my son going there was very exciting. But I could not imagine how my wife had managed to persuade a charity to pay for it, and when I asked her for the details so that I could write to them and thank them she replied that it was a secret charity.

"There are some charities which do not want to shout out their good deeds from the rooftops," she said. "They have asked me to tell nobody about this. But if you wish to thank them, you can write a letter, which I will deliver to them on your behalf."

I wrote this letter, but got no reply.

"They are far too busy to be writing to every parent they help," said my wife. "I don't see what you're complaining about. They're paying the fees, aren't they? Stop bothering them with all these letters."

There had only been one letter, but my wife always exaggerates things, at least when it concerns me. She accuses me of eating "hundreds of pumpkins, all the time", when I eat fewer pumpkins than she does. She says that I make more noise than an aeroplane when I snore, which is not true. She says that I am always spending money on my lazy nephew and sending him thousands of pula every year. In fact, I only give him one hundred pula on his birthday and one hundred pula for his Christmas box. Where she gets this figure of thousands of pula, I don't know. I also don't know where she gets all the money for her fashionable life. She tells me that she saves it, by being careful in the house, but I cannot see how it adds up. I will talk to you a little bit later about that.

But you must not misunderstand me, ladies. I am not one of these husbands who does not like his wife. I am very happy with my wife. Every day I reflect on how happy I am to be married to a fashionable lady – a lady who makes people look at her in the street. Many butchers are married to women who do not look very glamorous, but I am not one of those butchers. I am the butcher with the very glamorous wife, and that makes me proud.

I am also proud of my son. When he went to Thornhill he was behind in all his subjects and I was worried that they would put him down a year. But when I spoke to the teacher, she said that I should not worry about this, as the boy was very bright and would soon catch up. She said that bright children could always manage to get over earlier difficulties if they made up their mind to work.

My son liked the school. He was soon scoring top marks in mathematics and his handwriting improved so much that you would think it was a different boy writing. He wrote an essay which I have kept, "The causes of soil erosion in Botswana" and one day I shall show that to you, if you wish. It is a very beautiful piece of work and I think that if he carries on like this, he will one day become Minister of Mines or maybe Minister of Water Resources. And to think that he will get there as the grandson of a High Court orderly and the son of an ordinary butcher.

You must be thinking: *What has this man got to complain about? He has a fashionable wife and a clever son. He has got a butchery of his own. Why complain?* And I understand why one might think that, but that does not make me any more unhappy. Every night I wake up and think the same thought. Every day when I come back from work and find that my wife is not yet home, and I wait until ten or eleven o'clock before she returns, the anxiety gnaws away at my stomach like a hungry animal. Because, you see, *Bomma*, the truth of the matter is that I think my wife is seeing another man. I know that there are many husbands who say that, and they are imagining things, and I hope that I am just the same – just imagining – but I cannot have any peace until I know whether what I fear is true.

When Mr Letsenyane Badule eventually left, driving off in his rather battered Mercedes Benz, Mma Ramotswe looked at Mma Makutsi and smiled.

"Very simple," she said. "I think this is a very simple case, Mma Makutsi. You should be able to handle this case yourself with no trouble."

Mma Makutsi went back to her own desk, smoothing out the fabric of her smart blue dress. "Thank you, Mma. I shall do my best."

Mma Ramotswe nodded. "Yes," she went on. "A simple case of a man with a bored wife. It is a very old story. I read in a magazine that it is the sort of story that French people like to read. There is a story about a French lady called Mma Bovary, who was just like this, a very famous story. She was a lady who lived in the country and who did not like to be married to the same, dull man."

"It is better to be married to a dull man," said Mma Makutsi. "This Mma Bovary was very foolish. Dull men are very good husbands. They are always loyal and they never run away with other women. You are very lucky to be engaged to a ..."

She stopped. She had not intended it, and yet it was too late now. She did not consider Mr J.L.B. Matekoni to be dull; he was reliable, and he was mechanic, and he would be an utterly satisfactory husband. That is what she had meant; she did not mean to suggest that he was actually dull.

Mma Ramotswe stared at her. "To a what?" she said. "I am very lucky to be engaged to a what?"

Mma Makutsi looked down at her shoes. She felt hot and confused. The shoes, her best pair, the pair with the three glittering buttons stitched across the top, stared back at her, as shoes always do.

Then Mma Ramotswe laughed. "Don't worry," she said. "I know what you mean, Mma Makutsi. Mr J.L.B. Matekoni is maybe not the most fashionable man in town, but he is one of the best men there is. You could trust him with anything. He would never let you down. And I know he would never have any secrets from me. That is very important."

Grateful for her employer's understanding, Mma Makutsi was quick to agree.

'That is by far the best sort of man," she said. "If I am ever lucky enough to find a man like that, I hope he asks me to marry him."

She glanced down at her shoes again, and they met her stare. Shoes are realists, she thought, and they seemed to be saying: *No chance. Sorry, but no chance.*

"Well," said Mma Ramotswe. "Let's leave the subject of men in general and get back to Mr Badule. What do you think? Mr Andersen's book says that you must have a working supposition. You must set out to prove or disprove something. We have agreed that Mma Badule sounds bored, but do you think that there is more to it than that?"

Mma Makutsi frowned. "I think that there is something going on. She is getting money from somewhere, which means she is getting it from a man. She is paying the school fees herself with the money she has saved up."

Mma Ramotswe agreed. "So all you have to do is to follow her one day and see where she goes. She should lead you straight to this other man. Then you see how long she stays there, and you speak to the housemaid. Give her one hundred pula, and she will tell you the full story. Maids like to speak about the things that go on in their employers' houses. The employers often think that maids cannot hear, or see, even. They ignore them. And then, one day, they realise that the maid has been hearing and seeing all their secrets and is bursting to talk to the first person who asks her. That maid will tell you everything. You just see. Then you tell Mr Badule."

"That is the bit that I will not like," said Mma Makutsi. "All the rest I don't mind, but telling this poor man about this bad wife of his will not be easy."

Mma Ramotswe was reassuring. "Don't worry. Almost every time we detectives have to tell something like that to a client, the client already knows. We just provide the proof they are looking for. They know everything. We never tell them anything new."

"Even so," said Mma Makutsi. "Poor man. Poor man."

"Maybe," Mma Ramotswe added. "But remember, that for every cheating wife in Botswana, there are five hundred and fifty cheating husbands."

Mma Makutsi whistled. "That is an amazing figure," she said. "Where did you read that?"

"Nowhere," chuckled Mma Ramotswe. "I made it up.

But that doesn't stop it being true."

It was a wonderful moment for Mma Makutsi when she set forth on her first case. She did not have a driving licence, and so she had to ask her uncle, who used to drive a Government truck and who was now retired, to drive her on the assignment in the old Austin which he hired out, together with his services as driver, for weddings and funerals. The uncle was thrilled to be included on such a mission, and donned a pair of darkened glasses for the occasion.

They drove out early to the house beside the butchery, where Mr Badule and his wife lived. It was a slightly down-at-heel bungalow, surrounded by pawpaw trees, and with a silver-painted tin roof that needed attention. The yard was virtually empty, apart from the pawpaws and a wilting row of cannas along the front of the house. At the rear of the house, backed up against a wire fence that marked the end of the property, were the servant quarters and a lean-to garage.

It was hard to find a suitable place to wait, but eventually Mma Makutsi concluded that if they parked just round the corner, half-concealed by the small take-out stall that sold roast mealies, strips of fly-blown dried meat and, for those who wanted a real treat, delicious pokes of mopani worms. There was no reason why a car should not park there; it would be a good place for lovers to meet, or for somebody to wait for the arrival of a rural relative off one of the rickety buses that careered in from the Francistown Road.

The uncle was excited, and lit a cigarette.

"I have seen many films like this," he said. "I never dreamed that I would be doing this work, right here in Gaborone."

"Being a private detective is not all glamorous work," said his niece. "We have to be patient. Much of our work is just sitting and waiting."

"I know," said the uncle. "I have seen that on films too. I have seen these detective people sit in their cars and eat sandwiches while they wait. Then somebody starts shooting."

Mma Makutsi raised an eyebrow. "There is no shooting in Botswana," she said. "We are a civilized country."

They lapsed into a companionable silence, watching people set about their morning business. At seven o'clock the door of the Badule house opened and a boy came out, dressed in the characteristic uniform of Thornhill School. He stood for a moment in front of the house, adjusting the strap of his school satchel, and then walked up the path that led to the front gate.

Then he turned smartly to the left and strode down the road.

"That is the son," said Mma Makutsi, lowering her voice, although nobody could possibly hear them. "He has a scholarship to Thornhill School. He is a bright boy, with very good handwriting."

The uncle looked interested.

"Should I write this down?" he asked. "I could keep a record of what happens."

Mma Makutsi was about to explain that this would not be necessary, but she changed her mind. It would give him something to do, and there was no harm in it. So the uncle wrote on a scrap of paper that he had extracted from his pocket: "Badule boy leave house at 7 a.m. and proceeds to school on foot."

He showed her his note, and she nodded.

"You would make a very good detective, Uncle," she said, adding: "It is a pity you are too old."

Twenty minutes later, Mr Badule emerged from the house and walked over to the butchery. He unlocked the door and admitted his two assistants, who had been waiting for him under a tree. A few minutes later, one of the assistants, now wearing a heavily blood-stained apron, came out carrying a large stainless steel tray, which he washed under a stand-pipe at the side of the building. Then two customers arrived, one having walked up the street, another getting off a minibus which stopped just beyond the take-out stall.

"Customers enter shop," wrote the Uncle. "Then leave, carrying parcels. Probably meat."

Again he showed the note to his niece, who nodded approvingly.

"Very good. Very useful. But it is the lady we are interested in," she said. "Soon it will be time for her to do something."

They waited a further four hours. Then, shortly before twelve, when the car had become stiflingly hot under the sun, and just at the point when Mma Makutsi was becoming irritated by her uncle's constant note-taking, they saw Mma Badule emerge from behind the house and walk over to the garage. There she got into the battered Mercedes Benz and reversed out of the front drive. This was the signal for the uncle to start his car and, at a respectful distance, follow the Mercedes as it made its way into town.

Mma Badule drove fast, and it was difficult for the uncle to keep up with her in his old Austin, but they still had her in sight by the time that she drew into the driveway of a large house on Nyerere Drive. They drove past slowly, and caught a glimpse of her getting out of the car and striding towards the shady verandah. Then the luxuriant garden growth, so much richer than the miserable pawpaw trees at the butchery house, obscured their view.

But it was enough. They drove slowly round the corner and parked under a jacaranda tree at the side of the road.

"What now?" asked the uncle. "Do we wait here until she leaves."

Mma Makutsi was uncertain. "There is not much point in sitting here," she said. "We are really interested in what is going on in that house."

She remembered Mma Ramotswe's advice. The best source of information was undoubtedly the maids, if they could be persuaded to talk. It was now lunchtime, and the maids would be busy in the kitchen. But in an hour or so, they would have their own lunch break, and would come back to the servants' quarters. And those could be reached quite easily, along the narrow sanitary lane that ran along the back of the properties. That would be the time to speak to them and to offer the crisp new fifty pula notes with which Mma Ramotswe had issued her the previous evening.

The uncle wanted to accompany her, and Mma Makutsi had difficulty persuading him that she could go alone.

"It could be dangerous," he said. "You might need protection."

She brushed aside his objections. "Dangerous, Uncle? Since when has it been dangerous to talk to a couple of maids in the middle of Gaborone, in the middle of the day?"

He had had no answer to that, but he nonetheless looked anxious when she left him in the car and made her way along the lane to the back gate. He watched her hesitate behind the small, white-washed building which formed the servants' quarters, before making her way round to the door, and then he lost sight of her. He took out his pencil, glanced at the time, and made a note: Mma Makutsi enters servants' quarters at 2.10p.m.

There were two of them, just as she had anticipated. One of them was older than the other, and had crow's-feet wrinkles at the side of her eyes. She was a comfortable, large-chested woman, dressed in a green maid's dress and a pair of scuffed white shoes of the sort which nurses wear. The younger woman, who looked as if she was in her mid-twenties, Mma Makutsi's own age, was wearing a red house coat and had a sultry, spoiled face. In other clothes, and made-up, she would not have looked out of place as a bar girl. Perhaps she is one, thought Mma Makutsi.

The two woman stared at her, the younger one quite rudely.

"Ko ko," said Mma Makutsi, politely, using the greeting that could substitute for a knock when there was no door to be knocked upon. This was necessary, as although the women were not inside their house they were not quite outside either, being seated on two stools in the cramped open porch at the front of the building.

The older woman studied their visitor, raising her hand to shade her eyes against the harsh light of the early afternoon.

"Dumela, Mma. Are you well?"

The formal greetings were exchanged, and then there was silence. The younger woman poked at their small, blackened kettle with a stick.

"I wanted to talk to you, my sisters," said Mma Makutsi. "I want to find out about that woman who has come to visit this house, the one who drives that Mercedes Benz. You know that one?"

The younger maid dropped the stick. The older one nodded. "Yes, we know that woman."

"Who is she?"

The younger retrieved her stick and looked up at Mma Makutsi. "She is a very important lady, that one! She comes to the house and sits in the chairs and drinks tea. That is who she is."

The other one chuckled. "But she is also a very tired lady," she said. "Poor lady, she works so hard that she has to go and lie down in the bedroom a lot, to regain her strength."

The younger one burst into a peal of laughter. "Oh yes," she said. "There is much resting done in that bedroom. He helps her to rest her poor legs. Poor lady."

Mma Makutsi joined in their laughter. She knew immediately that this was going to be much easier than she had imagined it would be. Mma Ramotswe was right, as usual; people liked to talk, and, in particular, they liked to talk about people who annoyed them in some way. All one had to do was to discover the grudge and the grudge itself would do all the work. She felt in her pocket for the two fifty pula notes; it might not even be necessary to use them after all. If this were the case, she might ask Mma Ramotswe to authorise their payment to her uncle.

"Who is the man who lives in this house?" she said. "Has he no wife of his own?"

This was the signal for them both to giggle. "He has a wife all right," said the older one. "She lives out at their village, up near Mahalaype. He goes there at weekends. This lady here is his town wife."

"And does the country wife know about this town wife?"

"No," said the older woman. "She would not like it. She is a Catholic woman, and she is very rich. Her father had four shops up there and bought a big farm. Then they came and dug a big mine on that farm and so they had to pay that woman a lot of money. That is how she bought this big house for her husband. But she does not like Gaborone."

"She is one of those people who never likes to leave the village," the younger maid interjected. 'There are some people like that. She lets her husband live here to run some sort of business that she owns down here. But he has to go back every Friday, like a schoolboy going home for the weekend"

Mma Makutsi looked at the kettle. It was a very hot day, and she wondered if they would offer her tea. Fortunately the older maid noticed her glance and made the offer.

"And I'll tell you another thing," said the younger maid as she lit the paraffin stove underneath the kettle. "I would write a letter to the wife and tell her about that other woman, if I were not afraid that I would lose my job."

"He told us," said the other. "He said that if we told his

wife, then we would lose our jobs immediately. He pays us well, this man. He pays more than any other employer on this whole street. So we cannot lose this job. We just keep our mouths shut ..."

She stopped, and at that moment both maids looked at one another in dismay.

"Aiee!" wailed the younger one. "What have we been doing? Why have we spoken like this to you? Are you from Mahalaype? Have you been sent by the wife? We are finished! We are very stupid women. Aiee!"

"No," said Mma Makutsi quickly. "I do not know the wife. I have not even heard of her. I have been asked to find out by that other woman's husband what she is doing. That is all."

The two maids became calmer, but the old one still looked worried. "But if you tell him what is happening, then he will come and chase this man away from his own wife and he might tell the real wife that her husband has another woman. That way we are finished too. It makes no difference."

"No," said Mma Makutsi. "I don't have to tell him what is going on. I might just say that she is seeing some man but I don't know who it is. What difference does it make to him? All he needs to know is that she is seeing a man. It does not matter which man it is."

The younger maid whispered something to the other, who frowned.

"What was that, Mma?" asked Mma Makutsi.

The older one looked up at her. "My sister was just wondering about the boy. You see, there is a boy, who belongs to that smart woman. We do not like that woman, but we do like the boy. And that boy, you see, is the son of this man, not of the other man. They both have very big noses. There is no doubt about it. You take a look at them and you will see it for yourself. This one is the father of that boy, even if

[129]

the boy lives with the other one. He comes here every afternoon after school. The mother has told the boy that he must never speak to his other father about coming here, and so the boy keeps this thing secret from him. That is bad. Boys should not be taught to lie like that. What will become of Botswana, Mma, if we teach boys to behave like that. Where will Botswana be if we have so many dishonest boys? God will punish us, I am sure of it. Aren't you?"

Mma Makutsi looked thoughtful when she returned to the Austin in its shady parking place. The uncle had dropped off to sleep, and was dribbling slightly at the side of his mouth. She touched him gently on the sleeve and he awoke with a start.

"Ah! You are safe! I am glad that you are back."

"We can go now," said Mma Makutsi. "I have found out everything I needed to know."

They drove directly back to the No .1 Ladies' Detective Agency. Mma Ramotswe was out, and so Mma Makutsi paid her uncle with one of the fifty pula notes and sat down at her desk to type her report.

"The client's fears are confirmed," she wrote. 'His wife has been seeing the same man for many years. He is the husband of a rich woman, who is also a Catholic. The rich woman does not know about this. The boy is the son of this man, and not the son of the client. I am not sure what to do, but I think that we have the following choices:

(a) We tell the client everything that we have found out. That is what he has asked us to do. If we do not tell him this, then perhaps we would be misleading him. By taking on this case, have we not promised to tell him everything? If that is so, then we must do so, because we must keep our promises. If we do not keep our promises, then there will be no difference between Botswana and ~~Nigeria~~ a certain other country in Africa which I do not want to name here but which I know you know.

(b) We tell the client that there is another man, but we do not know who it is. This is strictly true, because I did not find out the name of the man, although I know which house he lives in. I do not like to lie, as I am a lady who believes in God. But God sometimes expects us to think about what the results will be of telling somebody something. If we tell the client that that boy is not his son, he will be very sad. It will be like losing a son. Will that make him happier? Would God want him to be unhappy?

And if we tell the client this, and there is a big row, then the father may not be able to pay the school fees, as he is doing at present. The rich woman may stop him from doing that and then the boy will suffer. He will have to leave that school.

For these reasons, I do not know what to do."

She signed the report and put it on Mma Ramotswe's desk. Then she stood up and looked out of the window, over the acacia trees and up into the broad, heat-drained sky. It was all very well being a product of the Botswana Secretarial College, and it was all very well having graduated with 97 per cent. But they did not teach moral philosophy there, and she had no idea how to resolve the dilemma with which her successful investigation had presented her. She would leave that to Mma Ramotswe. She was a wise woman, with far more experience of life than herself, and she would know what to do.

Mma Makutsi made herself a cup of bush tea and stretched out in her chair. She looked at her shoes, with their three twinkling buttons. Did they know the answer? Perhaps they did.

A *Trip into Town*

O N THE MORNING of Mma Makutsi's remarkably success ful, but nonetheless puzzling investigation into the affairs of Mr Letsenyane Badule, Mr J.L.B. Matekoni, proprietor of Tlokweng Road Speedy Motors, and undoubtedly one of the finest mechanics in Botswana, decided to take his newly-acquired foster children into town on a shopping expedition. Their arrival in his house had confused his ill-tempered maid, Mma Florence Peko, and had plunged him into a state of doubt and alarm that at times bordered on panic. It was not everyday that one went to fix a diesel pump and came back with two children, one of them in a wheel-chair, saddled with an implied moral obligation to look after the children for the rest of their childhood, and, indeed, in the case of the wheelchair-bound girl, for the rest of her life. How Mma Silvia Potokwane, the ebullient matron of the orphan farm, had managed to persuade him to take the children was beyond him. There had been some sort of conversation about it, he knew, and he had said that he would do it, but how had he been pushed into committing himself there and then? Mma Potokwane was like a clever lawyer engaged in the examination of a witness: agreement would be obtained to some innocuous statement and then, before the witness knew it, he would have agreed to a quite different proposal.

But the children had arrived, and it was now too late to do anything about it. As he sat in the office of Tlokweng Road Speedy Motors and contemplated a mound of paperwork, he made two decisions. One was to employ a secretary

– a decision which he knew, even as he took it, that he would never get round to implementing – and the second was to stop worrying about how the children had arrived and to concentrate on doing the right thing by them. After all, if one contemplated the situation in a calm and detached state of mind, it had many redeeming features. The children were fine children – you only had to hear the story of the girl's courage to realise that – and their life had taken a sudden and dramatic turn for the better. Yesterday they had been just two of one hundred and fifty children at the orphan farm. Today they were placed in their own house, with their own rooms, and with a father – yes, he was a father now! – who owned his own garage. There was no shortage of money; although not a conspicuously wealthy man, Mr J.L.B. Matekoni was perfectly comfortable. Not a single *thebe* was owed on the garage; the house was subject to no bond; and the three accounts in Barclays Bank of Botswana were replete with pula. Mr J.L.B. Matekoni could look any member of the Gaborone Chamber of Commerce in the eye and say: " I have never owed you a penny. Not one." How many businessmen could do that these days? Most of them existed on credit, kow-towing to that smug Mr Timon Mothokoli, who controlled business credit at the bank. He had heard that Mr Mothokoli could drive to work form his house on Kaunda Way and would be guaranteed to drive past the doors of at least five men who would quake at his passing. Mr J.L.B. Matekoni could, if he wished, ignore Mr Mothokoli if he met him in the Mall, not that he would ever do that, of course.

So if there is all this liquidity, thought Mr J.L.B. Matekoni, then why not spend some of it on the children? He would arrange for them to go to school, of course, and there was no reason why they should not go to a private school, too. They would get good teachers there; teachers who knew all about Shakespeare and geometry. They would learn everything that they needed to get good jobs. Perhaps the boy ... No, it was almost to much to hope for, but it was such a delicious thought. Perhaps the boy would demonstrate an aptitude for mechanical matters and could take over the running of Tlokweng Road Speedy Motors. For a few moments, Mr J.L.B. Matekoni indulged himself in the thought: his son, his *son*, standing in front of the garage, wiping his hands on a piece of oily rag, after having done a good job on a complicated gearbox. And, in the background, sitting in the office, himself and Mma Ramotswe, much older now, grey-haired, drinking bush tea.

That would be far in the future, and there was much to be done before that happy outcome could be achieved. First of all, he would take them into town and buy them new clothes. The orphan farm, as usual, had been generous in giving them going-away clothes that were nearly new, but it was not the same as having one's own clothes, bought from a shop. He imagined that these children had never had that luxury. They would never have unwrapped clothes from their factory packaging and put them on, with that special, quite unreproducible smell of new fabric rich in the nostrils. He would drive them in immediately, that very morning, and buy them all the clothes they needed. Then he would take them to the chemist shop and the girl could buy herself some creams and shampoo, and other things that girls might like for themselves. There was only carbolic soap at home, and she deserved better than that.

Mr J.L.B. Matekoni fetched the old green truck from the garage, which had plenty of room in the back for the wheelchair. The children were sitting on the verandah when he arrived home; the boy had found a stick which he was tying up in string for some reason, and the girl was crocheting a cover for a milk jug. They taught them crochet at the orphan farm, and some of them had won prizes for their designs. She is a talented girl, thought Mr J.L.B. Matekoni; this girl will be able to do anything, once she is given the chance.

They greeted him politely, and nodded when he asked whether the maid had given them their breakfast. He had asked her to come in early so as to be able to attend to the children while he went off to the garage, and he was slightly surprised that she had complied. But there were sounds from the kitchen – the bangings and scrapings that she seemed to make whenever she was in a bad mood – and these confirmed her presence.

Watched by the maid, who sourly followed their progress until they were out of sight near the old Botswana Defence Force Club, Mr J.L.B. Matekoni and the two children bumped their way into town in the old truck. The springs were gone, and only be replaced with difficulty, as the manufacturers had passed into mechanical history, but the engine still worked and the bumpy ride was a thrill for the girl and boy. Rather to Mr J.L.B. Matekoni's surprise, the girl showed an interest in its history, asking him how old it was and whether it used a lot of oil.

"I have heard that old engines need more oil," she said. "Is this true, Rra?'

Mr J.L.B. Matekoni explained about worn engine parts and their heavy demands, and she listened attentively. The boy, by contrast, did not appear to be interested. Still, there was time. He would take him to the garage and get the apprentices to show him how to take off wheel nuts. That was a task that a boy could perform, even when he was as young as this one. It was best to start early as a mechanic. It was an art which, ideally, one should learn at one's father's side. Did not the Lord himself learn to be a carpenter in his father's workshop? Mr J.L.B. Matekoni thought. If the Lord came back today, he would probably be a mechanic, he reflected.

[135]

That would be a great honour for mechanics everywhere. And there is no doubt but that he would choose Africa: Israel was far too dangerous these days. In fact, the more one thought about it, the more likely it was that he would choose Botswana, and Gaborone in particular. Now that would be a wonderful honour for the people of Botswana; but it would not happen, and there was no point in thinking about it any further. The Lord was not going to come back; we had had our chance and we had not made very much of it, unfortunately.

He parked the car beside the British High Commission, noting that His Excellency's white Range Rover was in front of the door. Most of the diplomatic cars went to the big garages, with their advanced diagnostic equipment and their exotic bills, but His Excellency insisted on Mr J.L.B. Matekoni.

"You see that car over there?" said Mr J.L.B. Matekoni to the boy. "That is a very important vehicle. I know that car very well."

The boy looked down at the ground and said nothing.

"It is a beautiful white car," said the girl, from behind him. "It is like a cloud with wheels."

Mr J.L.B. Matekoni turned round and looked at her.

"That is a very good way of talking about that car," he said. "I shall remember that."

"How many cylinders does a car like that have?" the girl went on. "Is it six?"

Mr J.L.B. Matekoni smiled, and turned back to the boy. "Well," he said. "How many cylinders do you think that car has in its engine?"

"One?" said the boy quietly, still looking firmly at the ground.

"One!" mocked his sister. "It is not a two-stroke!"

Mr J.L.B. Matekoni's eyes opened wide. "A two stroke?

Where did you hear about two-strokes?"

The girl shrugged. "I have always known about two-strokes," she said. "They make a loud noise and you mix the oil in with the petrol. They are mostly on small motorbikes. Nobody likes a two-stroke engine."

Mr J.L.B. Matekoni nodded. "No, a two stroke engine is often very troublesome." He paused. "But we must not stand here and talk about engines. We must go to the shops and buy you clothes and other things that you need."

The shop assistants were sympathetic to the girl, and went with her into the changing room to help her try the dresses which she had selected from the rack. She had modest tastes, and consistently chose the cheapest available, but these, she said, were the ones she wanted. The boy appeared more interested; he chose the brightest shirts he could find and set his heart on a pair of white shoes which his sister vetoed on the grounds of impracticality.

"We cannot let him have those, Rra," she said to Mr J.L.B. Matekoni. "They would get very dirty in no time and then he will just throw them to one side. This is a very vain boy."

"I see," mused Mr J.L.B. Matekoni thoughtfully. The boy was respectful, and presentable, but that earlier delightful image he had entertained of his son standing outside Tlokweng Road Speedy Motors seemed to have faded. Another image had appeared, of the boy in a smart white shirt and a suit ... But that could not be right.

They finished their shopping and were making their way back across the broad public square outside the post office when the photographer summoned them.

"I can do a photograph for you," he said. "Right here. You stand under this tree and I can take your photograph. Instant. Just like that. A handsome family group."

"Would you like that?" asked Mr J.L.B. Matekoni "A

photograph to remind us of our shopping trip."

The children beamed up at him.

"Yes, please," said the girl, adding, "I have never had a photograph."

Mr J.L.B. Matekoni stood quite still. This girl, now in her early teens, had never had a photograph of herself. There was no record of her childhood, nothing which would remind her of what she used to be. There was nothing, no image, of which she could say: "That is me". And all this meant that there was nobody who had ever wanted her picture; she had simply not been special enough.

He caught his breath, and for a moment, he felt an overwhelming rush of pity for these two children; and pity mixed with love. He would give them these things. He would make it up to them. They would have everything that other children had been given, which other children took for granted; all that love, each year of lost love, would be replaced, bit by bit, until the scales were righted.

He wheeled the wheelchair into position in front of the tree where the photographer had established his outdoor studio. Then, his rickety tripod perched in the dust, the photographer crouched behind his camera and waved a hand to attract his subject's attention. There was a clicking sound, following by a whirring, and with the air of a magician completing a trick, the photographer peeled off the protective paper and blew across the photograph to dry it.

The girl took it, and smiled. Then the photographer positioned the boy, who stood, hands clasped behind him, mouth wide open in a smile; again the theatrical performance with the print and the pleasure on the child's face.

"There," said Mr J.L.B. Matekoni. "Now you can put those in your rooms. And one day we will have more photographs."

He turned round and prepared to take control of the wheelchair, but he stopped, and his arms fell to his sides, useless, paralysed.

There was Mma Ramotswe, standing before him, a basket laden with letters in her right hand. She had been making her way to the post office when she saw him and she had stopped. What was going on? What was Mr J.L.B. Matekoni doing, and who were these children?

The Sullen, Bad Maid Acts

FLORENCE PEKO, THE sour and complaining maid of Mr J.L.B. Matekoni, had suffered from headaches ever since Mma Ramotswe had first been announced as her employer's future wife. She was prone to stress headaches, and anything untoward could bring them on. Her brother's trial, for instance, had been a season of headaches, and every month, when she went to visit him in the prison near the Indian supermarket she would feel a headache even before she took her place in the shuffling queue of relatives waiting to visit. Her brother had been involved in stolen cars, and although she had given evidence on his behalf, testifying to having witnessed a meeting at which he had agreed to look after a car for a friend – a skein of fabrication – she knew that he was every bit as guilty as the prosecution had made him out to be. Indeed, the crimes for which he received his five-year prison sentence were probably only a fraction of those he had committed. But that was not the point: she had been outraged at his conviction, and her outrage had taken the form of a prolonged shouting and gesturing at the police officers in the court. The magistrate, who was on the point of leaving, had resumed her seat and ordered Florence to appear before her.

"This is a court of law," she had said. "You must understand that you cannot shout at police officers, or anybody else in it. And moreover, you are lucky that the prosecutor has not charged you with perjury for all the lies you told here today."

Florence had been silenced, and had been allowed free.

Yet this only increased her sense of injustice. The Republic of Botswana had made a great mistake in sending her brother to jail. There were far worse people than he, and why were they left untouched? Where was the justice of it if people like … The list was a long one, and, by curious coincidence, three of the men on it were known by her, two of them intimately.

And it was to one of these, Mr Philemon Leannye, that she now proposed to turn. He owed her a favour. She had once told the police that he was with her, when he was not, and this was after she had received her judicial warning for perjury and was wary of the authorities. She had met Philemon Leannye at a take-out stall in the African Mall. He was tired of bar girls, he had said, and he wanted to get to know some honest girls who would not take his money from him and make him buy drinks for them.

"Somebody like you," he had said, charmingly.

She had been flattered, and their acquaintance had blossomed. Months might go by when she would not see him, but he would appear from time to time and bring her presents – a silver clock once, a bag (with the purse still in it), a bottle of Cape Brandy. He lived over at Old Naledi, with a woman by whom he had had three children.

"She is always shouting at me, that woman," he complained. "I can't do anything right as far as she is concerned. I give her money every month but she always says that the children are hungry and how is she to buy the food? She is never satisfied."

Florence was sympathetic.

"You should leave her and marry me," she said. "I am not one to shout at a man. I would make a good wife for a man like you."

Her suggestion had been serious, but he had treated it as a joke, and had cuffed her playfully.

"You would be just as bad," he said. "Once women are

[141]

married to men, they start to complain. It is a well-known fact. Ask any married man."

So their relationship remained casual, but, after her risky and rather frightening interview with the police – an interview in which his alibi was probed for over three hours – she felt that there was an obligation which one day could be called in.

"Philemon,' she said to him, lying beside him on Mr J.L.B. Matekoni's bed one hot afternoon. "I want you to get me a gun."

He laughed, but became serious when he turned over and saw her expression.

"What are you planning to do? Shoot Mr J.L.B. Matekoni? Next time he comes into the kitchen and complains about the food, you shoot him? Hah!"

"No. I am not planning to shoot anybody. I want the gun to put in somebody's house. Then I will tell the police that there is a gun there and they will come and find it."

"And so I don't get my gun back?'

"No. The police will take it. But they will also take the person whose house it was in. What happens if you are found with an illegal gun?"

Philemon lit a cigarette and puffed the air straight up towards Mr J.L.B. Matekoni's ceiling.

"They don't like illegal weapons here. You get caught with an illegal gun and you go to prison. That's it. No hanging about. They don't want this place to become like Johannesburg."

Florence smiled. "I am glad that they are so strict about guns. That is what I want."

Philemon extracted a fragment of tobacco from the space between his two front teeth. "So," he said. "How do I pay for this gun? Five hundred pula. Minimum. Somebody has to bring it over from Johannesburg. You can't pick them up here so easily."

"I have not got five hundred pula," she said. "Why not steal the gun. You've got contacts. Get one of your boys to do it." She paused before continuing. "Remember that I helped you. That was not easy for me."

He studied her carefully. "You really want this?"

"Yes," she said. "It's really important to me."

He stubbed his cigarette out and swung his legs over the edge of the bed.

"All right," he said. "I'll get you a gun. But remember that if anything goes wrong, you didn't get the gun from me."

"I shall say I found it," said Florence. "I shall say that it was lying in the bush over near the prison. Maybe it was something to do with the prisoners."

"Sound reasonable," said Philemon. "When do you want it?"

"As soon as you can get it," she replied.

"I can get you one tonight," he said. "As it happens, I have a spare one. You can have that."

She sat up and touched the back of his neck gently. "You are a very kind man. You can come and see me any time, you know. Any time. I am always happy to see you and make you happy."

"You are a very fine girl," he said, laughing. "Very bad. Very wicked. Very clever."

He delivered the gun, as he had promised, wrapped in a wax-proof parcel, which he put at the bottom of a voluminous OK Bazaars plastic bag, underneath a cluster of old copies of *Ebony* magazine. She unwrapped it in his presence and he started to explain how the safety catch operated, but she cut him short.

"I'm not interested in that," she said. "All I'm interested in is this gun, and these bullets."

He had handed her, separately, nine rounds of stubby, heavy ammunition. The bullets shone, as if each had been polished for its task, and she found herself attracted to their feel. They would make a fine necklace, she thought, if drilled through the base and threaded through with nylon string or perhaps a silver chain.

Philemon showed her how to load bullets into the magazine and how to wipe the gun afterwards, to remove fingerprints. Then he gave her a brief caress, planted a kiss on her cheek, and left. The smell of his hair oil, an exotic rum-like smell, lingered in the air, as it always did when he visited her, and she felt a stab of regret for their languid afternoon and its pleasures. If she went to his house and shot his wife, would he marry her? Would he see her as his liberator, or the slayer of the mother of his children? It was difficult to tell.

Besides, she could never shoot anybody. She was a Christian, and she did not believe in killing people. She thought of herself as a good person, who was simply forced, by circumstances, to do things that good people did not do – or which they claimed they did not do. She knew better, of course. Everybody cut some corners, and if she was proposing to deal with Mma Ramotswe in this unconventional way, it was only because it was necessary to use such measures against somebody who was so patently a threat to Mr J.L.B. Matekoni. How could he defend himself against a woman as determined as that? It was clear that strong steps be taken, and a few years in prison would teach that woman to be more respectful of the rights of others. That interfering detective woman was the author of her own misfortune; she only had herself to blame.

Now, thought Florence, I have obtained a gun. This gun must now be put into the place that I have planned for it, which is a certain house in Zebra Drive.

To do this, another favour had to be called in. A man known to her simply as Paul, a man who came to her for conversation and affection, had borrowed money from her two years previously. It was not a large sum, but he had never paid it back. He might have forgotten about it, but she had not, and now he would be reminded. And if he proved difficult, he, too, had a wife who did not know about the social visits that her husband paid to Mr J.L.B. Matekoni's house. A threat to reveal these might encourage compliance.

It was money, though, that had secured agreement. She mentioned the loan, and he stuttered out his inability to pay.

"Every pula I have has to be accounted for," he said. "We have to pay the hospital for one of the children. He keeps getting ill. I cannot spare any money. I will pay you back one day."

She nodded her understanding. "It will be easy to forget," she said. "I shall forget this money if you do something for me."

He had stared at her suspiciously. "You go to an empty house – nobody will be there. You break a window in the kitchen and you get in."

"I am not a thief," he interrupted. "I do not steal."

"But I am not asking you to steal," she said. "What kind of thief goes into a house and puts something into it? That is not a thief!"

She explained that she wanted a parcel left in a cupboard somewhere, tucked away where it could not be found.

"I want to keep something safe," she said. "This thing will be safe there."

He had cavilled at the idea, but she mentioned the loan again, and he capitulated. He would go the following afternoon, at a time when everybody was at work. She had done her homework: there would not even be a maid at the house, and there was no dog.

"It couldn't be easier," she promised him. "You will get it done in fifteen minutes. In. Out."

She handed him the parcel. The gun had been replaced in its wax-proof paper and this had been itself wrapped in a further layer of plain brown paper. The wrapping disguised the nature of the contents, but the parcel was still weighty and he was suspicious.

"Don't ask,' she said. "Don't ask and then you won't know."

It's a gun, he thought. She wants me to plant a gun in that house in Zebra Drive.

"I don't want to carry this thing about with me," he said. "It is very dangerous. I know that it's a gun and I know what happens to you if the police find you with a gun. I do not want to go to jail. I will fetch it from you at the Matekoni house tomorrow."

She thought for a moment. She could take the gun with her to work, tucked away in a plastic bag. If he wished to fetch it from her from there, then she had no objection. The important thing was to get it into the Ramotswe house and then, two days later, to make that telephone call to the police.

"All right,' she said. "I will put it back in its bag and take it with me. You come at two thirty. He will have gone back to his garage by then."

He watched her replace the parcel in the OK Bazaars bag in which it had first arrived.

"Now,' she said. "You have been a good man and I want to make you happy."

He shook his head. "I am too nervous to be happy. Maybe some other time."

The following afternoon, shortly after two o'clock, Paul Monsopati, a senior clerk at the Gaborone Sun Hotel, and a man marked by the hotel management for further promotion, slipped into the office of one of the hotel secretaries and asked her to leave the room for a few minutes.

"I have an important telephone call to me," he said. "It is a private matter. To do with a funeral."

The secretary nodded, and left the room. People were always dying and funerals, which were eagerly attended by every distant relative who was able to do so, and by almost every casual acquaintance, required a great deal of planning.

Paul picked up the telephone receiver and dialled a number which he had written out on a piece of paper.

"I wish to speak to an Inspector,' he said. "Not a sergeant. I want an Inspector."

"Who are you, Rra?"

"That is not important. You get me an Inspector, or you will be in trouble."

Nothing was said, and, after a few minutes, a new voice came on the line.

"Now listen to me, please, Rra," said Paul. "I cannot speak for long. I am a loyal citizen of Botswana. I am against crime."

"Good," said the Inspector. 'That is what we like to hear."

"Well," said Paul. "If you go to a certain house you will find that there is a lady there who has an illegal firearm. She is one who sells these weapons. It will be in a white OK Bazaars bag. You will catch her if you go right now. She is the one, not the man who lives in that house. It is in her bag, and she will have it with her in the kitchen. That is all I have to say."

He gave the address of the house and then rang off. At the other end of the line, the Inspector smiled with satisfaction. This would be an easy arrest, and he would be congratulated for doing something about illegal weapons. One might complain about the public and about their lack of a sense of duty, but every so often something like this happened and a conscientious citizen restored one's faith in ordinary members of the public. There should be awards for these people. Awards and a cash prize. Five hundred pula at least.

CHAPTER SIXTEEN

Family

M R J.L.B. Matekoni was aware of the fact that he was standing directly under the branch of an acacia tree. He looked up, and saw for a moment, in utter clarity, the details of the leaves against the emptiness of the sky. Drawn in upon themselves for the midday heat, the leaves were like tiny hands clasped in prayer; a bird, a common butcher bird, scruffy and undistinguished, was perched further up the branch, claws clasped tight, black eyes darting. It was the sheer enormity of Mr J.L.B. Matekoni's plight that made this perception so vivid; as a condemned man might peep out of his cell on his last morning and see the familiar, fading world.

He looked down, and saw that Mma Ramotswe was still there, standing some ten feet away, her expression one of bemused puzzlement. She knew that he worked for the orphan farm, and she was aware of Mma Silvia Potokwane's persuasive ways. She would be imagining, he thought, that here was Mr J.L.B. Matekoni taking two of the orphans out for the day and arranging for them to have their photographs taken. She would not be imagining that here was Mr J.L.B. Matekoni with his two new foster children, soon to be her foster children too.

Mma Ramotswe broke the silence. "What are you doing?" she said simply. It was an entirely reasonable question – the sort of question that any friend or indeed fiancée may ask of another. Mr J.L.B. Matekoni looked down at the children. The girl had placed her photograph in a plastic carrier bag that was attached to the side of her wheelchair; the boy was clutching his photograph to his chest, as if Mma Ramotswe might wish to take it from him.

"These are two children from the orphan farm," stuttered Mr J.L.B. Matekoni. "This one is the girl and this one is the boy."

Mma Ramotswe laughed. "Well!" she said. "So that is it. That is very helpful."

The girl smiled and greeted Mma Ramotswe politely.

"I am called Motholeli," she said. "My brother is called Puso. These are the names that we have been given at the orphan farm."

Mma Ramotswe nodded. "I hope that they are looking after you well, there. Mma Potokwane is a kind lady."

"She is kind," said the girl. "Very kind."

She looked as if she was about to say something else, and Mr J.L.B. Matekoni broke in rapidly.

"I have had the children's photographs taken," he explained, and turning to the girl, he said: "Show them to Mma Ramotswe, Motholeli."

The girl propelled her chair forward and passed the photograph to Mma Ramotswe, who admired it.

"That is a very nice photograph to have," she said. "I have only one or two photographs of myself when I was your age. If ever I am feeling old, I go and take a look at them and I think that maybe I am not so old after all."

"You are still young," said Mr J.L.B. Matekoni. "We are not old these days until we are seventy – maybe more. It has all changed."

"That's what we like to think," chuckled Mma Ramotswe, passing the photograph back to the girl. "Is Mr J.L.B. Matekoni taking you back now, or are you going to eat in town?"

"We have been shopping," Mr J.L.B. Matekoni blurted out. "We may have one or two other things to do."

"We will go back to his house soon," the girl said. "We

are living with Mr J.L.B. Matekoni now. We are staying in his house."

Mr J.L.B. Matekoni felt his heart thump wildly against his chest. I am going to have a heart attack, he thought. I am going to die now. And for a moment he felt immense regret that he would never marry Mma Ramotswe, that he would go to his grave a bachelor, that the children would be twice orphaned, that Tlokweng Road Speedy Motors would close. But his heart did not stop, but continued to beat, and Mma Ramotswe and all the physical world remained stubbornly there.

Mma Ramotswe looked quizzically at Mr J.L.B. Matekoni.

"They are staying in your house?" she said. "This is a new development. Have they just come?"

He nodded bleakly. "Yesterday," he said.

Mma Ramotswe looked down at the children and then back at Mr J.L.B. Matekoni.

"I think that we should have a talk," she said. "You children stay here for a moment. Mr J.L.B. Matekoni are going to the post office."

There was no escape. Head hanging, like a schoolboy caught in delinquency, he followed Mma Ramotswe to the corner of the post office, where before the stacked rows of private postal boxes, he faced the judgement and sentence that he knew were his lot. She would divorce him – if that was the correct term for the break-up of an engagement. He had lost her because of his dishonesty and stupidity – and it was all Mma Silvia Potokwane's fault. Women like that were always interfering in the lives of others, forcing them to do things; and then matters went badly astray and lives were ruined in the process.

Mma Ramotswe put down her basket of letters.

"Why did you not tell me about these children?" she asked.

"What have you done?'

He hardly dared meet her gaze. "I was going to tell you," he said. "I was out at the orphan farm yesterday. The pump was playing up. It's so old. Then their minibus needs new brakes. I have tried to fix those brakes, but they are always giving problems. We shall have to try and find new parts, I am have told them that, but ..."

"Yes, yes," pressed Mma Ramotswe. "You have told me about those brakes before. But what about these children?"

Mr J.L.B. Matekoni sighed. "Mma Potokwane is a very strong woman. She told me that I should take some foster children. I did not mean to do it without talking to you, but she would not listen to me. She brought in the children and I really had no alternative. It was very hard for me."

He stopped. A man passed on his way to his postal box, fumbling in his pocket for his key, muttering something to himself. Mma Ramotswe glanced at the man and then looked back at Mr J.L.B. Matekoni.

"So," she said, "you agreed to take these children. And now they think that they are going to stay."

"Yes, I suppose so," he mumbled.

"And how long for?" asked Mma Ramotswe.

Mr J.L.B. Matekoni took a deep breath. "For as long as they need a home," he said. "Yes, I offered them that."

Unexpectedly he felt a new confidence. He had done nothing wrong. He had not stolen anything, or killed anybody, or committed adultery. He had just offered to change the lives of two poor children who had had nothing and who would now be loved and looked after. If Mma Ramotswe did not like that, well there was nothing he could do about it now. He had been impetuous, but his impetuosity had been in a good cause.

Mma Ramotswe suddenly laughed. "Well, Mr J.L.B. Matekoni," she said. "Nobody could say of you that you are not a kind man. You are, I think, the kindest man in Botswana. What other man would do that? I do not know of one, not one single one. Nobody else would do that. Nobody."

He stared at her. "You are not cross?"

"I was," she said. "But only for a little while. One minute maybe. But then I thought: Do I want to marry the kindest man in the country? I do. Can I be a mother for them? I can. That is what I thought, Mr J.L.B. Matekoni."

He looked at her incredulously. "You are a very kind woman yourself, Mma. You have been very kind to me."

"We must not stand here and talk about kindness," she said. "There are those two children there. Let's take them back to Zebra Drive and show them where they are going to live. Then this afternoon I can come and collect them from your house and bring them to mine. Mine is more ..."

She stopped herself, but he did not mind.

"I know that Zebra Drive is more comfortable," he said. "And it would be better for them to be looked after by you."

They walked back to the children, together, companionably.

"I'm going to marry this lady," announced Mr J.L.B. Matekoni. "She will be your mother soon."

The boy looked startled, but the girl lowered her eyes respectfully.

"Thankyou, Mma," she said. "We shall try to be good children for you."

"That is good," said Mma Ramotswe. "We shall be a very happy family. I can tell it already."

Mma Ramotswe went off to fetch her tiny white van, taking the boy with her. Mr J.L.B. Matekoni pushed the girl's wheelchair back to the old truck, and the drove over to Zebra Drive, where Mma Ramotswe and Puso were already waiting for them by the time they arrived. The boy was excited, rushing out to greet his sister.

"This is a very good house," he cried out. "Look, there are trees, and melons. I am having a room at the back."

Mr J.L.B. Matekoni stood back as Mma Ramotswe showed the children round the house. Everything that he had felt about her was, in his mind, now confirmed beyond doubt. Obed Ramotswe, her father, who had brought her up after the death of her mother, had done a very fine job. He had given Botswana one of its finest ladies. He was a hero, perhaps without ever knowing it.

While Mma Ramotswe was preparing lunch for the children, Mr J.L.B. Matekoni telephoned the garage to check that the apprentices were managing to deal with the chores with which he had left them. The younger apprentice answered, and Mr J.L.B. Matekoni knew immediately from his tone that there was something seriously wrong. The young man's voice was artificially high and excited.

'I am glad that you telephoned, Rra," he said. "The police came. They wanted to speak to you about your maid. They have arrested her and she has gone off to the cells. She had a gun in her bag. They are very cross."

The apprentice had no further information, and so Mr J.L.B. Matekoni put down the receiver. His maid had been armed! He had suspected her of a great deal – of dishonesty, and possibly worse – but not of being armed. What was she up to in her spare time – armed robbery? Murder?

He went into the kitchen, where Mma Ramotswe was boiling up squares of pumpkin in a large enamel pot.

"My maid has been arrested and taken off to prison," he said flatly. "She had a gun. In a bag."

Mma Ramotswe put down her spoon. The pumpkin was boiling satisfactorily and would soon be tender. "I am not surprised," she said. "That was a very dishonest woman. The police have caught up with her at last. She was not too clever for them."

Mr J.L.B. Matekoni and Mma Ramotswe decided that after-noon that life was becoming too complicated for both of them and that they should declare the rest of the day to be a day of simple activities, centred around the children. To this end, Mr J.L.B. Matekoni telephoned the apprentices and told them to close the garage until the following morning.

"I have been meaning to give you time off to study," he said. "Well, you can have some study time this afternoon. Put up a sign and say that we shall re-open at eight tomor-row."

To Mma Ramotswe he said: "They won't study. They'll go off chasing girls. There is nothing in those young men's heads. Nothing."

"Many young people are like that," she said. "They think only of dances and clothes, and loud music. That is their life. We were like that too, remember?"

Her own telephone call to the No. 1 Ladies' Detective Agency had brought a confident Mma Makutsi to the line, who had explained to her that she had completed the inves-tigation of the Badule matter and that all that required to be done was to determine what to do with the information she had gathered. They would have to talk about that, said Mma Ramotswe. She had feared that the investigation would pro-duce a truth that would be far from simple in its moral implications. There were times when ignorance was more comfortable than knowledge.

The pumpkin, though, was ready, and it was time to sit down at the table, as a family for the first time.

Mma Ramotswe said grace.

"We are grateful for this pumpkin and this meat," she said. 'There are brothers and sisters who do not have good food on their table, and we think of them, and wish pump-kin and meat for them in the future. And we thank the Lord who has brought these children into our lives so that we might be happy and they might have a home with us. And we think of what a happy day this is for the late mother and the late daddy of these children, who are watching this from above."

Mr J.L.B. Matekoni could add nothing to this grace, which he thought was perfect in every respect. It expressed his own feelings entirely, and his heart was too full of emotion to allow him to speak. So he was silent.

CHAPTER SEVENTEEN

Seat of Learning

THE MORNING IS the best time to address a problem, thought Mma Ramotswe. One is at one's freshest in the first hours of the working day, when the sun is still low and the air is sharp. That is the time to ask oneself the major questions; a time of clarity and reason, unencumbered by the heaviness of the day.

"I have read your report," said Mma Ramotswe, when Mma Makutsi arrived for work. "It is a very full one, and very well written. Well done."

Mma Makutsi acknowledged the compliment graciously.

"I was happy that my first case was not a difficult one," she said. "At least it was not difficult to find out what needed to be found out. But those questions which I put at the end – they are the difficult bit."

"Yes," said Mma Ramotswe, glancing down at the piece of paper. "The moral questions."

"I don't know how to solve them," said Mma Makutsi. "If I think that one answer is correct, then I see all the difficulties with that. Then I consider the other answer, and I see another set of difficulties."

She looked expectantly at Mma Ramotswe, who grimaced.

"It is not easy for me either," the older woman said. "Just because I am a bit older than you does not mean that I have the answer to every dilemma that comes along. As you get older, in fact, you see more sides to a situation. Things are more clear-cut at your age." She paused, then added: "Mind you, remember that I am not quite forty. I am not all that old."

"No," said Mma Makutsi. "That is just about the right age for a person to be. But this problem we have; it is all very troubling. If we tell Badule about this man and he puts a stop to the whole thing, then the boy's school fees will not be paid. That will be the end of this very good chance that he is getting. That would not be best for the boy."

Mma Ramotswe nodded. "I see that," she said. "On the other hand we can't lie to Mr Badule. It is unethical for a detective to lie to the client. You can't do it."

"I can understand that," said Mma Makutsi. "But there are times, surely, when a lie is a good thing. What if a murderer came to your house and asked you where a certain person was? And what if you knew where that person was, would it be wrong to say: 'I do not know anything about that person. I do not know where he is.' Would that not be a lie?"

"Yes. But then you have no duty to tell the truth to that murderer. So you can lie to him. But you do have a duty to tell the truth to your client, or to your spouse, or to the police. That is all different."

"Why? Surely if it is wrong to lie, then it is always wrong to lie. If people could lie when they thought it was the right thing to do, then we could never tell when they meant it." Mma Makutsi, stopped, and pondered for a few moments before continuing. "One person's idea of what is right may be quite different from another's. If each person can make up his own rule..." She shrugged, leaving the consequences unspoken.

"Yes," said Mma Ramotswe. "You are right about that. That's the trouble with the world these days. Everyone thinks that they can make their own decisions about what is right and wrong. Everybody thinks that they can forget the old Botswana morality. But they can't."

"But the real problem here," said Mma Makutsi, "is whether we should tell him everything. What if we say: 'You are right; your wife is unfaithful,' and leave it at that? Have we done our duty? We are not lying, are we. We are just not telling all the truth."

Mma Ramotswe stared at Mma Makutsi. She had always valued her secretary's comments, but she had never expected that she would make such a moral mountain out of the sort of little problem that detectives encountered every day. It was messy work. You helped other people with their problems; you did not have to come up with a complete solution. What they did with the information was their own affair. It was their life, and they had to lead it.

But as she thought about this, she realised that she had done far more than that in the past. In a number of her successful cases, she had gone beyond the finding of information. She had made decisions about the outcome, and these decisions had often proved to be momentous ones. For example, in the case of the woman whose husband had a stolen Mercedes Benz, she had arranged for the return of the car to its owner. In the case of the fraudulent insurance claims by the man with thirteen fingers, she had made the decision not to report him to the police. That was a decision which had changed a life. He may have become honest after she had given him this chance, but he may not. She could not tell. But what she had done was to offer him a chance, and that may have made a difference. So she did interfere in other people's lives, and it was not true that all that she did was provide information.

In this case, she realised that the real issue was the fate of the boy. The adults could look after themselves; Mr Badule could cope with a discovery of adultery (in his heart of hearts he already knew that his wife was unfaithful); the other man could go back to his wife on his bended knees and take his punishment (perhaps be hauled back to live in that remote village with his Catholic wife), and as for the fashionable lady, well, she could spend a bit more time in the butchery, rather than resting on that big bed on Nyerere Drive. The boy, though, could not be left to the mercy of events. She would have to ensure that whatever happened, he did not suffer for the bad behaviour of his mother.

Perhaps there was a solution which would mean that the boy could stay at school. If one looked at the situation as it stood, was there anybody who was really unhappy? The fashionable wife was very happy; she had a rich lover and a big bed to lie about in. The rich lover bought her fashionable clothes and other things which fashionable ladies tend to enjoy. The rich lover was happy, because he had a fashionable lady and he did not have to spend too much time with his devout wife. The devout wife was happy because she was living where she wanted to live, presumably doing what she liked doing, and had a husband who came home regularly, but not so regularly as to be a nuisance to her. The boy was happy, because he had two fathers, and was getting a good education at an expensive school.

That left the Mr Letsenyane Badule? Was he happy, or if he was unhappy could he be made to be happy again without any change in the situation? If they could find some way of doing that, then there was no need for the boy's circumstances to change. But how might this be achieved? She could not tell Mr Badule that the boy was not his – that would be too upsetting, too cruel, and presumably the boy would be upset to learn this as well. It was probable that the boy did not realize who his real father was; after all, even if they had identical large noses, boys tend not to notice things like that and he may have thought nothing of it. Mma Ramotswe decided that there was no need to do anything about that; ignorance was probably the best state for the boy. Later on, with his school fees all paid, he could start to study family noses and draw his own conclusions.

"It's Mr Badule," Mma Ramotswe pronounced. "We have to make him happy. We have to tell him what is going on, but we must make him accept it. If he accepts it, then the whole problem goes away."

"But he's told us that he worries about it," objected Mma Makutsi.

"He worries because he thinks it is a bad thing for his wife to be seeing another man," Mma Ramotswe countered. "We shall persuade him otherwise."

Mma Makutsi looked doubtful, but was relieved that Mma Ramotswe had taken charge again. No lies were to be told, and, if they were, they were not going to be told by her. Anyway, Mma Ramotswe was immensely resourceful. If she believed that she could persuade Mr Badule to be happy, then there was a good chance that she could.

But there were other matters which required attention. There had been a letter from Mrs Curtin in which she asked whether Mma Ramotswe had unearthed anything. "I know it's early to be asking," she wrote, "but ever since I spoke to you, I have had the feeling that you would discover something for me. I don't wish to flatter you, Mma, but I had the feeling that you were one of these people who just *knew*. You don't have to reply to this letter; I know I should not be writing it at this stage, but I have to do something. You'll understand, Mma Ramotswe – I know you will."

The letter had touched Mma Ramotswe, as did all the pleas that she received from troubled people. She thought of the progress that had been made so far. She had seen the place and she had sensed that that was where that young man's life had ended. In a sense, then, she had reached the conclusion right at the beginning. Now she had to work backwards and find out why he was lying there – as she knew he was – in that dry earth, on the edge of the Great Kalahari. It was a lonely grave, so far away from his people, and he had been so young. How had it come to this? Wrong had been done at some point, and if one wanted to find out what wrong had occurred, then one had to find the people who were capable of doing that wrong. Mr Oswald Ranta.

The tiny white van moved gingerly over the speed bumps which were intended to deter fast and furious driving by the university staff. Mma Ramotswe was a considerate driver and was ashamed of the bad driving which made the roads so perilous. Botswana, of course, was much safer than other countries in that part of Africa. South Africa was very bad; there were aggressive drivers there, who would shoot you if you crossed them, and they were often drunk, particularly after pay day. If pay day fell on a Friday night, then it was foolhardy to set out on the roads at all. Swaziland was even worse. The Swazis loved speed, and the winding road between Manzini and Mbabane, on which she had once spent a terrifying half hour, was a notorious claimant of motoring life. She remembered coming across a poignant item in an odd copy of *The Times of Swaziland*, which had displayed a picture of a rather mousy-looking man, small and insignificant, under which was printed the simple legend *The late Mr Richard Mavuso (46)*. Mr Mavuso, who had a tiny head and a small, neatly-trimmed moustache, would have been beneath the notice of most beauty queens and yet, unfortunately, as the newspaper report revealed, he had been run over by one.

Mma Ramotswe had been strangely affected by the report. *Local man, Mr Richard Mavuso (above) was run over on Friday night by the Runner-up to Miss Swaziland. The well-known Beauty Queen, Miss Gladys Lapelala, of Manzini, ran over Mr Mavuso as he was trying to cross the road in Mbabane, where he was a clerk in the Public Works Department.*

That was all that the report had said, and Mma Ramotswe wondered why she was so affected by it. People were being run over all the time, and not much was made of it. Did it make a difference that one was run over by a beauty queen? And was it sad because Mr Mavuso was such a small and insignificant man, and the beauty queen so big, and important? Perhaps such an event was a striking metaphor for life's injustices; the powerful, the glamorous, the fêted, could so often with impunity push aside the insignificant, the timorous.

She nosed the tiny white van into a parking space behind the Administration Buildings and looked about her. She passed the university grounds every day, and was familiar with the cluster of white, sun-shaded buildings that sprawled across the several hundred-acre sight near the old air field. Yet she had never had the occasion to set foot there, and now, faced with a rather bewildering array of blocks, each with its impressive, rather alien name, she felt slightly overawed. She was not an uneducated woman, but she had no B.A. And this was a place where everybody one came across was either a B.A. or B.Sc. or even more than that. There were unimaginably learned people here; scholars like Professor Tlou, who had written a history of Botswana and a biography of Seretse Khama. Or there was Dr Bojosi Otloghile, who had written a book on the High Court of Botswana, which she had bought, but not yet read. One might come across such a person turning a corner in one of these buildings and they would look just like anybody else. But their heads would contain rather more than the heads of the average person, which were not particularly full of very much for a great deal of the time.

She looked at a board which proclaimed itself a map of the campus. Department of Physics that way; Department of

Theology that way; Institute of Advanced Studies first right. And then, rather more helpfully, Inquiries. She followed the arrow for Inquiries and came to a modest, prefabricated building, tucked away behind Theology and in front of African Languages. She knocked at the door and entered.

An emaciated woman was sitting behind a desk, trying to unscrew the cap of a pen.

"I am looking for Mr Ranta," she said. "I believe he works here."

The woman looked bored. "Dr Ranta," she said. "He is not just plain Mr Ranta. He is Dr Ranta."

"I am sorry," said Mma Ramotswe. "I would not wish to offend him. Where is he, please?"

"They seek him here, they seek him there," said the woman. "He is here one moment, the next moment, he is nowhere. That's Dr Ranta."

"But will he be here at this moment?" said Mma Ramotswe. "I am not worried about the next moment."

The woman arched an eyebrow. "You could try his office. He has an office here. But most of the time he spends in his bedroom."

"Oh," said Mma Ramotswe. "He is a ladies' man, this Dr Ranta?"

"You could say that," said the woman. "And one of these days the University Council will catch him and tie him up with rope. But in the meantime, nobody dares touch him."

Mma Ramotswe was intrigued. So often, people did one's work for one, as this woman was now doing.

"Why can people not touch him?' asked Mma Ramotswe.

"The girls themselves are too frightened to speak," said the woman. "And his colleagues all have something to hide themselves. You know what these places are like."

Mma Ramotswe shook her head. "I am not a B.A.," she

said. "I do not know."

"Well," said the woman, "I can tell you. They have a lot of people like Dr Ranta in them. You'll find out. I can speak to you about this because I'm leaving tomorrow. I'm going to a better job."

Mma Ramotswe was given instructions as to how to find Dr Ranta's office and she took her leave of the helpful receptionist. It was not a good idea on the university's part, she thought, to put that woman in the inquiry office. If she greeted any inquiry as to a member of staff with the gossip on that person, a visitor might get quite the wrong impression. Yet perhaps it was just because she was leaving the next day that she was talking like this; in which case, thought Mma Ramotswe, there was an opportunity.

"One thing, Mma," she said, as she reached the door. "It may be hard for anybody to deal with Dr Ranta because he hasn't done anything wrong. It may not be a good thing to interfere with students, but that may not be grounds for sacking him, at least it may not be these days. So maybe there's nothing that can be done."

She saw immediately that it was going to work, and that her surmise, that the receptionist had suffered at the hands of Dr Ranta, was correct.

"Oh yes, he has," she retorted, becoming suddenly animated. "He showed an examination paper to a student if she would oblige him. Yes! I'm the only one who knows it. The student was my cousin's daughter. She spoke to her mother, but she would not report it. But the mother told me."

"But you have no proof?" said Mma Ramotswe, gently. "Is that the problem?"

"Yes," said the receptionist. "There is no proof. He would lie his way out of it."

"And this girl, this Margaret, what did she do?"

"Margaret? Who is Margaret?"

"Your cousin's daughter," said Mma Ramotswe.

"She is not called Margaret," said the receptionist. "She is called Angel. She did nothing, and he got away with it. Men get away with it, don't they? Every time."

Mma Ramotswe felt like saying *No. Not always*, but she was short of time, and so she said goodbye for the second time and began to make her way to the Department of Economics.

The door was open. Mma Ramotswe looked at the small notice before she knocked: *Dr Oswald Ranta, B.Sc. (Econ.),(UB) Ph.D. (Duke). If I am not in, you may leave a message with the Departmental Secretary. Students wishing to have essays returned should see their tutor or go to the Departmental Office.*

She listened for the sound of voices from within the room and none came. She heard the click of the keys of a keyboard. Dr Ranta was in.

He looked up sharply as she knocked and edged the door open.

"Yes, Mma,' he said. "What do you want?"

Mma Ramotswe switched from English to Setswana. "I would like to speak to you, Rra. Have you got a moment."

He glanced quickly at his watch.

"Yes," he said, not impolitely. "But I haven't got forever. Are you one of my students?'

Mma Ramotswe made a self-deprecating gesture as she sat down on the chair which he had indicated. "No," she said. "I am not that educated. I did my Cambridge Certificate, but nothing after that. I was busy working for my cousin's husband's bus company, you see. I could not go on with my education."

'It is never too late, Mma," he said. "You could study. We have some very old students here. Not that you are very old, of course, but the point is that anybody can study."

"Maybe," she said. "Maybe one day."

"You could study just about anything here," he went on. "Except medicine. We can't make doctors just yet."

"Or detectives."

He looked surprised. "Detectives? You cannot study detection at a university."

She raised an eyebrow. "But I have read that at American universities there are courses in private detection. I have a book by ..."

He cut her short. "Oh that! Yes, at American colleges you can take a course in anything. Swimming, if you like. But that's only at some of them. At the good places, places that we call Ivy League, you can't get away with that sort of nonsense. You have to study real subjects."

"Like logic?"

"Logic? Yes. You would study that for a philosophy degree. They taught logic at Duke, of course. Or they did when I was there."

He expected her to look impressed, and she tried to oblige him with a look of admiration. This, she thought, is a man who needs constant reassurance – hence all the girls.

"But surely that is what detection is all about. Logic, and a bit of psychology. If you know logic, you know how things should work; if you know psychology, you should know how people work."

He smiled, folding his hands across his stomach, as if preparing for a tutorial. As he did so, his gaze was running down Mma Ramotswe's figure, and she sensed it. She looked back at him, at the folded hands, and the sharp dresser's tie.

"So, Mma," he said. "I would like to spend a long time discussing philosophy with you. But I have a meeting soon and I must ask you to tell me what you wanted to talk about. Was it philosophy after all?"

She laughed. 'I would not waste your time, Rra. You are a clever man, with many committees in your life. I am just a lady detective. I ..."

She saw him tense. The hands unfolded, and moved to the arms of the chair.

"You are a detective?" he asked. The voice was colder now.

She made a self-deprecating gesture. "It is only a small agency. The No.1 Ladies' Detective Agency. It is over by Kgale Hill. You may have seen it."

"I do not go over there," he said. "I have not heard of you."

"Well, I wouldn't expect you to have heard of me, Rra. I am not well known, unlike you."

His right hand moved uneasily to the knot of his tie.

"Why do you want to talk to me?" he asked. "Has somebody told you to come and speak to me?"

"No," she said. "It's not that."

She noticed that her answer relaxed him and the arrogance returned.

"Well then?" he said.

"I have come to ask you to talk about something that happened a long time ago. Ten years ago."

He stared at her. His look was guarded now, and she smelt off him that unmistakeable, acrid smell of a person experiencing fear.

"Ten years is a long time. People do not remember."

"No," she conceded. "They forget. But there are some things that are not easily forgotten. A mother, for example, will not forget her son."

As she spoke, his demeanour changed again. He got up from his chair, laughing.

"Oh," he said. "I see now. That American woman, the one who is always asking questions, is paying you to go round digging up the past again. Will she never give up? Will she never learn?"

"Learn what?" asked Mma Ramotswe.

He was standing at the window, looking out on a group of students on the walkway below.

"Learn that there is nothing to be learned," he said. "That boy is dead. He must have wandered off into the Kalahari and got lost. Gone for a walk and never come back. It's easily done, you know. One thorn tree looks much like another, you know, and there are no hills down there to guide you. You get lost. Especially if you're a white man out of your natural element. What do you expect?"

"But I don't believe that he got lost and died," said Mma Ramotswe. "I believe that something else happened to him."

He turned to face her.

"Such as?" he snapped.

She shrugged her shoulders. "I am not sure exactly what. But how should I know? I was not there." She paused, before adding, almost under her breath. "You were."

She heard his breathing, as he returned to his chair. Down below, one of the students shouted something out, something about a jacket, and the others laughed.

"You say I was there. What do you mean?"

She held his gaze. "I mean that you were living there at the time. You were one of the people who saw him every day. You saw him on the day of his death. You must have some idea."

"I told the police at the time, and I have told the Americans who came round asking questions of all of us. I saw him that morning, once, and then again at lunchtime. I told them what we had for lunch. I described the clothes he was wearing. I told them everything."

As he spoke, Mma Ramotswe made her decision. He was lying. Had he been telling the truth, she would have brought the encounter to an end, but she knew now that her initial intuition had been right. He was lying as he spoke. It was easy to tell; indeed, Mma Ramotswe could not understand why everybody could not tell when another person was lying. In her eyes, it was so obvious, and Dr Ranta might as well have had an illuminated liar sign about his neck.

"I do not believe you, Rra," she said simply. "You are lying to me."

He opened his mouth slightly, and then closed it. Then, folding his hands over his stomach again, he leant back in his chair.

"Our talk has come to an end, Mma," he announced. "I am sorry that I cannot help you. Perhaps you can go home and study some more logic. Logic will tell you that when a person says he cannot help you, you will get no help. That, after all, is logical."

He spoke with a sneer, pleased with his elegant turn of phrase.

"Very well, Rra," sad Mma Ramotswe. "You could help me, or rather you could help that poor American woman. She is a mother. You had a mother. I could say to you, *Think about that mother's feelings*, but I know that with a person like you that makes no difference. You do not care about that woman. Not just because she is a white woman, from far away; you wouldn't care if she was a woman from your own village, would you?"

He grinned at her. "I told you. We have finished our talk."

"But people who don't care about others can sometimes be made to care," she said.

He snorted. "In a minute I am going to telephone the Administration and tell them that there is a trespasser in my room. I could say that I found you trying to steal something. I could do that, you know. In fact, I think that is just what I might do. We have had trouble with casual thieves recently and they would send the security people pretty quickly. You might have difficulty explaining it all, Mrs Logician."

"I wouldn't do that, Rra," she said. "You see, I know all about Angel."

The effect was immediate. His body stiffened and again she smelled the acrid odour, stronger now.

"Yes," she said. "I know about Angel and the examination paper. I have a statement back in my office. I can pull the chair from under you now, right now. What would you do in Gaborone as an unemployed university lecturer, Rra? Go back to your village? Help with the cattle again?"

Her words, she noted, were like axe-blows. Extortion, she thought. Blackmail. This is how the blackmailer feels when he has his victim at his feet. Complete power.

"You cannot do that ... I will deny ... There is nothing to show ..."

"I have all the proof they will need," she said. "Angel, and another girl who is prepared to lie and say that you gave her exam questions. She is cross with you and she will lie. What she says is not true, but there will be two girls with the same story. We detectives call that corroboration, Rra. Courts like corroboration. They call it similar fact evidence. Your colleagues in the Law Department will tell you all about such evidence. Go and speak to them. They will explain the law to you."

He moved his tongue between his teeth, as if to moisten his lips. She saw that, and she saw the damp patch of sweat under his armpits; one of his laces was undone, she noted, and the tie had a stain, coffee or tea.

"I do not like doing this, Rra," she said. "But this is my job. Sometimes I have to be tough and do things that I do not like doing. But what I am doing now has to be done because there is a very sad American woman who only wants to say goodbye to her son. I know you don't care about her, but I do, and I think that her feelings are more important than yours. So I am going to offer you a bargain. You tell me what happened and I shall promise you – and my word means what it says, Rra – I shall promise you that we hear nothing more about Angel and her friend."

His breathing was irregular; short gasps, like that of a person with obstructive airways disease – a struggling for breath.

"I did not kill him," he said. "I did not kill him."

"Now you are telling the truth," said Mma Ramotswe. "I can tell that. But you must tell me what happened and where his body is. That is what I want to know."

"Are you going to go to the police and tell them that I withheld information? If you will, then I will just face whatever happens about that girl."

"No, I am not going to go to the police. This story is just for his mother. That is all."

He closed his eyes. "I cannot talk here. You can come to my house."

"I will come this evening."

"No," he said. "Tomorrow."

"I shall come this evening," she said. "That woman has waited ten years. She must not wait any longer."

"All right. I shall write down the address. You can come tonight at nine o'clock."

"I shall come at eight," said Mma Ramotswe. "Not every woman will do what you tell her to do, you know."

She left him, and as she made her way back to the tiny white van she listened to her own breathing and felt her own heart thumping wildly. She had no idea where she had found the courage, but it had been there, like the water at the bottom of a disused quarry – unfathomably deep.

CHAPTER EIGHTEEN

At Tlokweng Road Speedy Motors

WHILE MMA RAMOTSWE indulged in the pleasures of black mail – for that is what it was, even if in a good cause, and therein lay another moral problem which she and Mma Makutsi might chew over in due course – Mr J.L.B. Matekoni, *garagiste* to His Excellency, the British High Commissioner to Botswana, took his two foster children to the garage for the afternoon. The girl, Motholeli, had begged him to take them so that she could watch him work, and he, bemused, had agreed. A garage workshop was no place for children, with all those heavy tools and pneumatic hoses, but he could detail one of the apprentices to watch over them while he worked. Besides, it might be an idea to expose the boy to the garage at this stage so that he could get a taste for mechanics at an early age. An understanding of cars and engines had to be instilled early; it was not something that could be picked up later. One might become a mechanic at any age, of course, but not everybody could have a feeling for engines. That was something that had to be acquired by osmosis, slowly, over the years.

He parked in front of his office door so that Motholeli could get into the wheelchair in the shade. The boy dashed off immediately to investigate a tap at the side of the building and had to be called back.

"This place is dangerous," cautioned Mr J.L.B. Matekoni. "You must stay with one of these boys over there."

He called over the younger apprentice, the one who constantly tapped him on the shoulder with his greasy finger and ruined his clean overalls.

"You must stop what you are doing," he said. "You watch over these two while I am working. Make sure that they don't get hurt."

The apprentice seemed to be relieved by his new duties and beamed broadly at the children. He's the lazy one, thought Mr J.L.B. Matekoni. He would make a better nanny than a mechanic.

The garage was busy. There was a football team's minibus in for an overhaul and the work was challenging. The engine had been strained from constant overloading, but that was the case with every minibus in the country. They were always overloaded as the proprietors attempted to cram in every possible fare. This one, which needed new rings, had been belching acrid black smoke to the extent that the players were complaining about shortness of breath.

The engine was exposed and the transmission had been detached. With the help of the other apprentice, Mr J.L.B. Matekoni attached lifting tackle to the engine block and began to winch it out of the vehicle. Motholeli, watching intently from her wheelchair, pointed something out to her brother. He glanced briefly in the direction of the engine, but then looked away again. He was tracing a pattern in a patch of oil at his feet.

Mr J.L.B. Matekoni exposed the pistons and the cylinders. Then, pausing, he looked over at the children.

"What is happening now, Rra?" called the girl. "Are you going to replace those rings there? What do they do? Are they important?'

Mr J.L.B. Matekoni looked at the boy. "You see, Puso? You see what I am doing?"

The boy smiled weakly.

"He is a drawing a picture in the oil," said the apprentice. "He is drawing a house."

The girl said: "May I come closer, Rra?" she said. "I will

not get in the way."

Mr J.L.B. Matekoni nodded and, after she had wheeled herself across, he pointed out to her where the trouble lay.

"You hold this for me," he said. "There."

She took the spanner, and held it firmly.

"Good," he said. "Now you turn this one here. You see? Not too far. That's right."

He took the spanner from her and replaced it in his tray. Then he turned and looked at her. She was leaning forward in her chair, her eyes bright with interest. He knew that look; the expression of one who loves engines. It could not be faked; that younger apprentice, for example, did not have it, and that is why he would never be more than a mediocre mechanic. But this girl, this strange, serious child who had come into his life, had the makings of a mechanic. She had the art. He had never before seen it in a girl, but it was there. And why not? Mma Ramotswe had taught him that there is no reason why women should not do anything they wanted. She was undoubtedly right. People had assumed that private detectives would be men, but look at how well Mma Ramotswe had done. She had been able to use a woman's powers of observation and a woman's intuitions to find out things that could well escape a man. So if a girl might aspire to becoming a detective, then why should she not aspire to entering the predominantly male world of cars and engines?

Motholeli raised her eyes, meeting his gaze, but still respectfully.

"You are not cross with me, Rra?" she said. 'You do not think I am a nuisance?"

He reached forward and laid a hand gently on her arm.

"Of course I am not cross," he said. "I am proud. I am proud that now I have a daughter who will be a great mechanic. Is that what you want? Am I right?'

She nodded modestly. "I have always loved engines," she

[175]

said. "I have always liked to look at them. I have loved to work with screwdrivers and spanners. But I have never had the chance to do anything."

"Well," said Mr J.L.B. Matekoni. 'That changes now. You can come with me on Saturday mornings and help here. Would you like that? We can make a special workbench for you – a low one – so that it is the right height for your chair."

"You are very kind, Rra."

For the rest of the day, she remained at his side, watching each procedure, asking the occasional question, but taking care not to intrude. He tinkered and coaxed, until eventually the minibus engine, re-invigorated, was secured back in place and, when tested, produced no acrid black smoke.

"You see," said Mr J.L.B. Matekoni proudly, pointing to the clear exhaust. "Oil won't burn off like that if it's kept in the right place. Tight seals. Good piston rings. Everything in its proper place."

Motholeli clapped her hands. "That van is happier now," she said.

Mr J.L.B. Matekoni smiled. "Yes," he agreed. 'It is happier now."

He knew now, beyond all doubt, that she had the talent. Only those who really understood machinery could conceive of happiness in an engine; it was an insight which the non-mechanically minded simply lacked. This girl had it, while the younger apprentice did not. He would kick an engine, rather than talk to it, and he had often seen him forcing metal. You cannot force metal, Mr J.L.B. Matekoni had told him time after time. If you force metal, it fights back. Remember that if you remember nothing else I have tried to teach you. Yet the apprentice would still strip bolts by turning the nut the wrong way and would bend flanges if they seemed reluctant to fall into proper alignment. No machinery could be treated that way.

This girl was different. She understood the feelings of engines, and would be a great mechanic one day – that was clear.

He looked at her proudly, as he wiped his hands on cotton lint. The future of Tlokweng Road Speedy Motors seemed assured.

CHAPTER EIGHTEEN

What happened

MMA RAMOTSWE FELT afraid. She had experienced fear only once or twice before in her work as Botswana's only lady private detective (a title she still deserved; Mma Makutsi, it had to be remembered, was only an *assistant* private detective). She had felt this way when she had gone to see Charlie Gotso, the wealthy businessman who still cultivated witchdoctors, and indeed on that meeting she had wondered whether her calling might one day bring her up against real danger. Now, faced with going to Dr Ranta's house, the same cold feeling had settled in her stomach. Of course, there were no real grounds for this. It was an ordinary house in an everyday street near Maru-a-Pula School. There would be neighbours next door, and the sound of voices; there would be dogs barking in the night; there would be the lights of cars. She could not imagine that Dr Ranta would pose any danger to her. He was an accomplished seducer, perhaps, a manipulator, an opportunist, but not a murderer.

On the other hand, the most ordinary people can be murderers. And if this were to be the manner of one's death, then one was very likely to know one's assailant and meet him in very ordinary circumstances. She had recently taken out a subscription to the *Journal of Criminology* (an expensive mistake, because it contained little of interest to her) but among the meaningless tables and unintelligible prose she had come across an arresting fact: the overwhelming majority of homicide victims know the person who kills them. They are not killed by strangers, but by friends, family, work acquaintances. Mothers killed their children. Husbands killed their wives. Wives killed their husbands. Employees killed their employers. Danger, it seemed, stalked every interstice of day-to-day life. Could this be true? Not in Johannesburg, she thought, where people fell victim to *tsostis* who prowled about at night, to car thieves who were prepared to use their guns, and to random acts of indiscriminate violence by young men with no sense of the value of life. But perhaps cities like that were an exception; perhaps in more normal circumstances homicide happened in just this sort of surrounding – a quiet talk in a modest house, while people went about their ordinary business just a stone's throw away.

Mr J.L.B. Matekoni sensed that something was wrong. He had come to dinner, to tell her of his visit earlier that evening to his maid in prison, and had immediately noticed that she seemed distracted. He did not mention it at first; there was a story to tell about the maid, and this, he thought, might take Mma Ramotswe's mind off whatever it was that was preoccupying her.

"I have arranged for a lawyer to see her," he said. "There is a man in town who knows about this sort of case. I have arranged for him to go and see her in her cell and to speak for her in court."

Mma Ramotswe piled an ample helping of beans on Mr J.L.B. Matekoni's plate.

"Did she explain anything?" she asked. "It can't look good for her. Silly woman."

Mr J.L.B. Matekoni frowned. "She was hysterical when I first arrived. She started to shout at the guards. It was very embarrassing for me. They said: 'Please control your wife and tell her to keep her big mouth shut.' I had to tell them twice that she was not my wife."

"But why was she shouting?" asked Mma Ramotswe. "Surely she understands that she can't shout her way out of there."

"She knows that, I think," said Mr J.L.B. Matekoni. "She was shouting because she was so cross. She said that somebody else should be there, not her. She mentioned your name for some reason."

Mma Ramotswe placed the beans on her own plate. "Me? What have I got to do with this?"

"I asked her that," Mr J.L.B. Matekoni went on. "But she just shook her head and said nothing more about it."

"And the gun? Did she explain the gun?"

"She said that the gun didn't belong to her. She said that it belonged to a boyfriend and that he was coming to collect it. Then she said that she didn't know that it was there. She thought the parcel contained meat. Or so she claims."

Mma Ramotswe shook her head. "They won't believe that. If they did, then would they ever be able to convict anybody found in possession of an illegal weapon?'

"That's what the lawyer said to me over the telephone," said Mr J.L.B. Matekoni. "He said that it was very hard to get somebody off one of these charges. The courts just don't believe them if they say that they didn't know there was a gun. They assume that they are lying and they send them to prison for at least a year. If they have previous convictions, and there usually are, then it can be much longer."

Mma Ramotswe raised her tea-cup to her lips. She liked to drink tea with her meals, and she had a special cup for the purpose. She would try to buy a matching one for Mr J.L.B. Matekoni, she thought, but it might be difficult, as this cup had been made in England and was very special.

Mr J.L.B. Matekoni looked sideways at Mma Ramotswe. There was something on her mind. In a marriage, he thought, it would be important not to keep anything from one's spouse, and they might as well start that policy now. Mind you, he recalled that had just kept the knowledge of two foster children from Mma Ramotswe, which was hardly a minor matter, but that was over now and a new policy could begin.

'Mma Ramotswe," he ventured. "You are uneasy tonight. Is it something I have said."

She put down her tea-cup, glancing at her watch as she did so.

"It's nothing to do with you," she said. "I have to go and speak to somebody tonight. It's about Mma Curtin's son. I am worried about this person I have to see."

She told him of her fears. She explained that although she knew that it was highly unlikely that an economist at the University of Botswana would turn to violence, nonetheless she felt convinced of the evil in his character, and this made her profoundly uneasy.

"There is a word for this sort of person," she explained. "I read about them. He is called a psychopath. He is a man with no morality."

He listened quietly, his brow furrowed with concern. Then, when she had finished speaking, he said: "You cannot go. I cannot have my future wife walking into danger like that."

She looked at him. "It makes me very pleased to know that you are worried about me," she said. "But I have my calling, which is that of a private detective. If I was going to be frightened, I should have done something else."

Mr J.L.B. Matekoni looked unhappy. "You do not know this man. You cannot go to his house, just like that. If you insist, then I shall come too. I shall wait outside. He need not know I am there."

Mma Ramotswe pondered. She did not want Mr J.L.B. Matekoni to fret, and if his presence outside would relieve his anxiety, then there was no reason why he should not come. "Very well," she said. "You wait outside. We'll take my van. You can sit there while I am talking to him."

"And if there is any emergency," he said. "You can shout. I shall be listening."

They both finished the meal in a more relaxed frame of mind. Motholeli was reading to her brother in his bedroom, the children having had their evening meal earlier. Dinner over, while Mr J.L.B. Matekoni took the plates through to the kitchen, Mma Ramotswe went down the corridor to find the girl half-asleep herself, the book resting on her knee. Puso was till awake, but drowsy, one arm across his chest, the other hanging down over the edge of the bed. She moved his arm back on to the bed and he smiled at her sleepily.

"It is time for you to go to bed too," she said to the girl. "Mr J.L.B. Matekoni tells me that you have had a busy day repairing engines."

She wheeled Motholeli back to her own room, where she helped her out of the chair and on to the side of the bed. She liked to have her independence, and so she allowed her to undress herself unaided and to get into the new nightgown that Mr J.L.B. Matekoni had bought for her on the shopping trip. It was the wrong colour, thought Mma Ramotswe, but then it had been chosen by a man, who could not be expected to know about these things.

"Are you happy here, Motholeli?" she asked.

"I am so happy," said the girl. "And every day my life is getting happier."

Mma Ramotswe tucked the sheet about her and planted a kiss on her cheek. Then she turned out the light and left the room. *Every day I am getting happier.* Mma Ramotswe wondered whether the world which this girl and her brother would inherit would be better than the world in which she and Mr J.L.B. Matekoni had grown up. They had grown happier, she thought, because they had seen Africa become independent and take its own steps in the world. But what a troubled adolescence the continent had experienced, with its vainglorious dictators and their corrupt bureaucracies. And all the time, African people were simply trying to lead decent lives in the midst of all the turmoil and disappointment. Did the people who made all the decisions in this world, the powerful people in places like Washington and London, know about people like Motholeli and Puso. Or care? She was sure that they would care, if only they knew. Sometimes she thought that people overseas had no room in their heart for Africa, because nobody had ever told them that African people were just the same as they were. They simply did not know about people like her Daddy, Obed Ramotswe, who stood, proudly attired in his shiny suit, in the photograph in her living room. You had no grandchildren, she said to the photograph, but now you have. Two. In this house.

The photograph was mute. He would have loved to have met the children, she thought. He would have been a good grandfather, who would have shown them the old Botswana morality and brought them to an understanding of what it is to live an honourable life. She would have to do that now; she and Mr J.L.B. Matekoni. One day soon she would drive out to the orphan farm and thank Mma Silvia Potokwane for giving them the children. She would also thank her for everything that she did for all those other orphans, because, she suspected, nobody ever thanked her for that. Bossy as Mma Potokwane might be, she was a matron, and it was a matron's job to be like that, just as detectives should be nosy, and mechanics ... Well, what should mechanics be? Greasy? No, greasy was not quite right. She would have to think further about that.

"I will be ready," said Mr J.L.B. Matekoni, his voice lowered, although there was no need. "You will know that I am here. Right here, outside the house. If you shout out, I will hear you."

They studied the house, in the dim light of the streetlamp, an undistinguished building with a standard red-tiled roof and unkempt garden.

"He obviously does not employ a gardener," observed Mma Ramotswe. "Look at the mess."

It was inconsiderate not to have a gardener if, like Dr Ranta, you were in a well-paid white-collar job. It was a social duty to employ domestic staff, who were readily available and desperate for work. Wages were low – unconscionably so, thought Mma Ramotswe – but at least the system created jobs. If everybody with a job had a maid, then that was food going into the mouths of the maids and their children. If everybody did their own housework and tended their own gardens, then what were the people who were maids and gardeners to do?

By not cultivating his garden, Dr Maeopi showed himself to be selfish, which did not surprise Mma Ramotswe at all.

"Too selfish," remarked Mr J.L.B. Matekoni.

"That's exactly what I was thinking," said Mma Ramotswe.

She opened the door of the van and manoeuvred herself out. The van was slightly too small for a lady like herself, of traditional build, but she was fond of it and dreaded the day when Mr J.L.B. Matekoni would be able to fix it no longer. No modern van, with all its gadgets and sophistication, would be able to take the place of the tiny white van. Since she had acquired it eleven years previously, it had borne her faithfully on her every journey, putting up with the heights of the October heat, or the fine dust which at certain times of year drifted in from the Kalahari and covered everything with a red-brown blanket. Dust was the enemy of engines, Mr J.L.B. Matekoni had explained – on more than one occasion – the enemy of engines, but the friend of the hungry mechanic.

Mr J.L.B. Matekoni watched Mma Ramotswe approach the front door and knock. Dr Ranta must have been waiting for her, as she was quickly admitted and the door was closed behind her.

"Is it just yourself, Mma?" said Dr Ranta. "Is your friend out there coming in?"

"No," she said. "He will wait for me outside."

Dr Ranta laughed. "Security? So you feel safe?"

She did not answer his question. 'You have a nice house," she said. "You are fortunate."

He gestured for her to follow him into the living room. Then he pointed to a chair and he himself sat down.

"I don't want to waste my time talking to you," he said. "I will speak only because you have threatened me and I am experiencing some difficulty with some lying women. That is the only reason why I am talking to you."

His pride was hurt, she realised. He had been cornered – and by a woman, too; a stinging humiliation for a womaniser. There was no point in preliminaries, she thought, and so she went straight to the point.

"How did Michael Curtin die?" she asked.

He sat in his chair, directly opposite her, his lips pursed.

"I worked there," he said, appearing to ignore her question. "I was a rural economist and they had been given a grant by the Ford Foundation to employ somebody to do studies of the economics of these small-scale agricultural ventures. That was my job. But I knew that things were hopeless. Right from the start. Those people were just idealists. They thought that you could change the way things had always been. I knew it wouldn't work."

"But you accepted the money," said Mma Ramotswe.

He stared at her contemptuously. "It was a job. I am a professional economist. I study things that work and things that don't work. Maybe you don't understand that."

"I understand," she said.

"Well," he went on. "We – the management, so to speak – lived in one large house. There was a German who was in charge of it – a man from Namibia, Burkhardt Fischer. He had a wife, Marcia, and then there was a South African woman, Carla Smit, the American boy and myself."

"We all got on quite well, except that Burkhardt did not like me. He tried to get rid of me shortly after I arrived, but I had a contract from the Foundation and they refused. He told lies about me, but they didn't believe him."

"The American boy was very polite. He spoke reasonable Setswana and people liked him. The South African woman took to him and they started to share the same room. She did everything for him – cooked his food, washed his clothes, and made a great fuss of him. Then she started to get interested in me. I didn't encourage her, but she had an affair with me, while she was still with that boy. She said to me that she was going to tell him, but that she didn't want to hurt his feelings. So we saw one another secretly, which was difficult to do out there, but we managed."

"Burkhardt suspected what was happening and he called me into his office and threatened that he would tell the American boy if I did not stop seeing Carla. I told him that it was none of his business, and he became angry. He said that he was going to write to the Foundation again and say that I was disrupting the work of the collective. So I told him that I would stop seeing Carla."

"But I did not. Why should I? We met one another in the evenings. She said that she liked going for walks in the bush in the dark; he did not like this, and he stayed. He warned her about going too far and about looking out for wild animals and snakes."

"We had a place where we went to be alone together. It was a hut beyond the fields. We used it for storing hoes and string and things like that. But it was also a good place for lovers to meet."

"That night we were in the hut together. There was full

moon, and it was quite light outside. I suddenly realised that somebody was outside the hut and I got up. I crept to the door and opened it very slowly. The American boy was outside. He was wearing just a pair of shorts and his veldschoens. It was a very hot night."

"He said: 'What are you doing here?' I said nothing, and he suddenly pushed past me and looked into the hut. He saw Carla there, and of course he knew straight away."

"At first he did not say anything. He just looked at her and then he looked at me. Then he began to run away from the hut. But he did not run back towards the house, but in the opposite direction, out into the bush."

"Carla shouted for me to go after him, and so I did. He ran quite fast, but I managed to catch up with him and I grabbed him by the shoulder. He pushed me off, and got away again. I followed him, even through thorn bushes, which were scratching at my legs and arms. I could easily have caught one of those thorns in my eye, but I did not. It was very dangerous.

"I caught him again, and this time he could not struggle so hard. I put my arms around him, to calm him down so that we could get him back to the house, but he fell away from me and he stumbled."

"We were at the edge of a deep ditch, a *donga*, that ran through the bush there. It was about six feet deep, and as he stumbled he fell down into the ditch. I looked down and saw him lying there on the ground. He did not move at all and he was making no sound."

"I climbed down and looked at him. He was quite still, and when I tried to look at his head to see if he had hurt it, it lolled sideways in my hand. I realised that he had broken his neck in the fall and that he was no longer breathing."

" I ran back to Carla and told her what had happened. She came with me back to the *donga* and we looked at him

[187]

again. He was obviously dead, and she started to scream."

"When she had stopped screaming, we sat down there in the ditch and wondered what to do. I thought that if we went back and reported what had happened, nobody would believe that he had slipped by accident. I imagined that people would say that he and I had had a fight after he discovered that I was seeing his girlfriend. I knew, in particular, that if the police spoke to Burkhardt, he would say bad things about me and would tell them that I had probably killed him. It would have looked very bad for me."

"So we decided to bury the body and to say that we knew nothing about it. I knew that there were anthills nearby; the bush there is full of them, and I knew that this was good place to get rid of a body. I found one quite easily, and I was lucky. An ant-eater had made quite a large hole in the side of one of the mounds, and I was able to enlarge this slightly and then put the body in. Then I stuffed in stones and earth and swept around the mound with a branch of a thorn tree. I think that I must have covered all traces of what had happened, because the tracker that they got in picked up nothing. Also, there was rain the next day, and that helped to hide any signs."

"The police asked us questions over the next few days, and there were other people, too. I told them that I had not seen him that evening, and Carla said the same thing. She was shocked, and became very quiet. She did not want to see me any more, and she spent a lot of her time crying."

"Then Carla left. She spoke to me briefly before she went, and she told me that she was sorry that she had become involved with me. She also told me that she was pregnant, but that the baby was his, not mine because she must already have been pregnant by the time she and I started seeing one another."

"She left, and then I left one month later. I was given a

scholarship to Duke; she left the country. She did not want to go back to South Africa, which she didn't like. I heard that she went up to Zimbabwe, to Bulawayo, and that she took a job running a small hotel there. I heard the other day that she is still there. Somebody I know was in Bulawayo and he said that he had seen her in the distance."

He stopped and looked at Mma Ramotswe. "That is the truth, Mma," he said. "I didn't kill him. I have told you the truth."

Mma Ramotswe nodded. "I can tell that," she said. "I can tell that you were not lying." She paused. "I am not going to say anything to the police. I told you that, and I do not go back on my word. But I am going to tell the mother what happened, provided that she makes the same promise to me – that she will not go to the police, and I think that she will give me that promise. I do not see any point in the police re-opening the case."

It was clear that Dr Ranta was relieved. His expression of hostility had gone now, and he seemed to be seeking some sort of reassurance from her.

"And those girls," he said. "They won't make trouble for me?"

Mma Ramotswe shook her head. "There will be no trouble from them. You need not worry about that."

"What about that statement?" he asked. "The one from that other girl? Will you destroy it."

Mma Ramotswe rose to her feet and moved towards the door.

"That statement?"

"Yes," he said. "The statement about me from the girl who was lying."

Mma Ramotswe opened the front door and looked out. Mr J.L.B. Matekoni was sitting in the car and looked up when the front door was opened.

She stepped down onto the pathway.

"Well, Dr Ranta," she said quietly. " I think that you are a man who has lied to a lot of people, particularly, I think, to women. Now something has happened which you may not have had happen to you before. A woman has lied to you and you have fallen for it entirely. You will not like that, but maybe it will teach you what it is to be manipulated. There was no girl."

She walked down the path and out of the gate. He stood at the door watching her, but she knew that he would not dare do anything. When he got over the anger which she knew he would be feeling, he would reflect that she had let him off lightly, and, if he had the slightest vestige of a conscience he might also be grateful to her for setting to rest the events of ten years ago. But she had her doubts about his conscience, and she thought that this, on balance, might be unlikely.

As for her own conscience: she had lied to him and she had resorted to blackmail. She had done so in order to obtain information which she otherwise would not have got. But again that troubling issue of means and ends raised its head. Was it right to do the wrong thing to get the right result? Yes, it must be. There were wars which were just wars. Africa had been obliged to fight to liberate itself, and nobody said that it was wrong to use force to achieve that result. Life was messy, and sometimes there was no other way. She had played Dr Ranta at his own game, and had won, just as she had used deception to defeat that cruel witchdoctor in her earlier case. It was regrettable, but necessary in a world that was far from perfect.

CHAPTER NINETEEN

Bulawayo

LEAVING EARLY, WITH the town barely stirring and the sky still in darkness, she drove in the tiny white van out on to the Francistown Road. Just before she reached the Mochudi turn-off, where the road ambled down to the source of the Limpopo, the sun began to rise above the plains, and for a few minutes, the whole world was a pulsating yellow-gold – the *kopjes,* the panoply of the tree tops, last season's dry grass beside the road, the very dust. The sun, a great red ball, seemed to hang above the horizon and then freed itself and floated up over Africa; the natural colours of the day returned, and Mma Ramotswe saw in the distance the familiar roofs of her childhood, and the donkeys beside the road, and the houses dotted here and there among the trees.

This was a dry land, but now, at the beginning of the rainy season, it was beginning to change. The early rains had been good. Great purple clouds had stacked up to the north and east, and the rain had fallen in white torrents, like a waterfall covering the land. The land, parched by months of dryness, had swallowed the shimmering pools which the downpour had created, and, within hours, a green tinge had spread over the brown. Shoots of grass, tiny yellow flowers, spreading tentacles of wild ground vines, broke through the softened crust of the earth and made the land green and lush. The waterholes, baked-mud depressions, were suddenly filled with muddy-brown water, and riverbeds, dry passages of sand, flowed again. The rainy season was the annual miracle which allowed life to exist in these dry lands – a miracle in which one had to believe, or the rains might never come, and the cattle might die, as they had done in the past.

She liked the drive to Francistown, although today she was going a further three hours north, over the border and into Zimbabwe. Mr J.L.B. Matekoni had been unwilling for her to go, and had tried to persuade her to change her mind, but she had insisted. She had taken on this enquiry, and she would have to see it through.

"It is more dangerous than Botswana," he had said. "There's always some sort of trouble up there. There was the war, and then the rebels, and then other troublemakers. Road-blocks. Hold-ups. That sort of thing. What if your van breaks down?"

It was a risk she had to take, although she did not like to worry him. Apart from the fact that she felt that she had to make the trip, it was important for her to establish the principle that she would make her own decisions on these matters. You could not have a husband interfering with the workings of the No 1 Ladies' Detective Agency; otherwise they might as well change the name to the No 1 Ladies' (and Husband) Detective Agency. Mr J.L.B. Matekoni was a good mechanic, but not a detective. It was a question of ... What was it? Subtlety? Intuition?

So the trip to Bulawayo would go ahead. She considered that she knew how to look after herself; so many people who got into trouble had only themselves to blame for it. They ventured into places where they had no business to be; they made provocative statements to the wrong people; they failed to read the social signals. Mma Ramotswe knew how to merge with her surroundings. She knew how to handle a young man with an explosive sense of his own importance, which was, in her view, the most dangerous phenomenon one might encounter in Africa. A young man with a rifle was a landmine; if you trod on his sensitivities – which was not hard to do – dire consequences could ensue. But if you handled him correctly – with the respect that such people crave – you might defuse the situation. But at the same time, you should not be too passive, or he would see you as an opportunity to assert himself. It was all a question of judging the psychological niceties of the situation.

She drove on through the morning. By nine o'clock she was passing through Mahalapye, where her father, Obed Ramotswe, had been born. He had moved south to Mochudi, which was her mother's village, but it was here that his people had been, and they were still, in a sense, her people. If she wandered about the streets of this haphazard town and spoke to old people, she was sure that she would find somebody who knew exactly who she was; somebody who could slot her into some complicated genealogy. There would be second, third, fourth cousins, distant family ramifications, that would bind her to people she had never met and among whom she would find an immediate sense of kinship. If the tiny white van were to break down, then she could knock on any one of those doors and expect, and receive, the help that distant relatives can claim among the Batswana.

Mma Ramotswe found it difficult to imagine what it would be like to have no people. There were, she knew, those who had no others in this life, who had no uncles, or aunts, or distant cousins of any degree; people who were *just themselves*. Many white people were like that, for some unfathomable reason; they did not seem to want to have people and were happy to be just themselves. How lonely they must be – like spacemen deep in space, floating in the darkness, but without even that silver, unfurling cord that linked the astronauts to their little metal womb of oxygen and warmth. For a moment, she indulged the metaphor, and imagined the tiny white van in space, slowly spinning against a background of stars and she, Mma Ramotswe, of the No. 1 Ladies' Space Agency, floating weightless, head over heels, tied to the tiny white van with a thin washing line.

She stopped at Francistown, and drank a cup of tea on the
verandah of the hotel overlooking the railway line. A diesel
train tugged at its burden of coaches, crowded with travel-
lers from the north, and shunted off; a goods train, laden
with copper from the mines of Zambia, stood idle, while its
driver stood and talked with a railways official under a tree.
A dog, exhausted by the heat, lame from a withered leg,
limped past. A child, curious, nose streaming, peeped round
a table at Mma Ramotswe, and then scuttled off giggling
when she smiled at him.

Now came the border crossing, and the slow shuffling
queue outside the white block in which the uniformed offi-
cials shuffled their cheaply-printed forms and stamped
passports and permissions, bored and officious at the same
time. The formalities over, she set out on the last leg of the
journey, past granite hills that faded into soft blue horizons,
through an air that seemed cooler, higher, fresher than the
oppressive heat of Francistown. And then into Bulawayo,
into a town of wide streets and jacaranda trees, and shady
verandahs. She had a place to stay here; the house of a friend
who visited her from time to time in Gaborone, and there
was a comfortable room awaiting her, with cold, polished
red floors and a thatch roof that made the air within as quiet
and as cool as the atmosphere in a cave.

"I am always happy to see you," said her friend. "But
why are you here?"

"To find somebody," said Mma Ramotswe. "Or rather,
to help somebody else to find somebody."

"You're talking in riddles," laughed her friend.

"Well, let me explain," said Mma Ramotswe. 'I'm here to
close a chapter."

She found her, and the hotel, without difficulty. Mma Ramotswe's friend made a few telephone calls and gave her the name and address of the hotel. It was an old building, in the colonial style, on the road to the Matopos. It was not clear who might stay there, but it seemed well kept and there was a noisy bar somewhere in the background. Above the front door, painted in small white lettering on black was a sign: *Carla Smit, Licensee, licensed to sell alcoholic beverages.* This was the end of the quest, and, as the end of a quest so often was, it was a mundane setting, quite unexceptionable; yet it was surprising nonetheless that the person sought should actually exist, and be there.

"I am Carla."

Mma Ramotswe looked at the woman, sitting behind her desk, an untidy pile of papers in front of her. On the wall behind her, pinned above a filing cabinet, was a year-chart with blocks of days marked up in bright colours; a gift from its printers, in heavy Bodoni type: *Printed by the Matabeleland Printing Company (Private) Limited: You think, we ink!* It occurred to her that she might issue a calendar to her own clients: *Suspicious? Call the No. 1 Ladies' Detective Agency. You ask, we answer!* No, that was too lame. *You cry, we spy!* No. Not all the clients felt miserable. *We find things out.* That was better: it had the necessary *dignity.*

"You are?" the woman enquired, politely, but with a touch of suspicion in her voice. She thinks that I have come for a job, thought Mma Ramotswe, and she is steeling herself to turn me down.

"My name is Precious Ramotswe," she said. "I'm from Gaborone. And I have not come to ask for a job."

The woman smiled. "So many people do," she said. "There is such terrible unemployment. People who have done all sorts of courses are desperate for a job. Anything. They'll do anything. I get ten, maybe twelve enquiries every week; many more at the end of the school year."

"Conditions are bad?"

The woman sighed. "Yes, and have been for some time. Many people suffer."

"I see," said Mma Ramotswe. "We are lucky down there in Botswana. We do not have these troubles."

Carla nodded, and looked thoughtful. "I know. I lived there for a couple of years. It was some time ago, but I hear it hasn't changed too much. That's why you are lucky."

"You preferred the old Africa?"

Carla looked at her quizzically. This was a political question, and she would need to be cautious.

She spoke slowly, choosing her words. "No. Not in the sense of preferring the colonial days. Of course not. Not all white people liked that, you know. I may have been a South African, but I left South Africa to get away from apartheid. That's why I went to Botswana."

Mma Ramotswe had not meant to embarrass her. Her question had not been a charged one, and she tried to set her at her ease. 'I didn't mean that," she said. "I meant the old Africa, when there were fewer people without jobs. People had a place then. They belonged to their village, to their family. They had their lands. Now a lot of that has gone and they have nothing but a shack on the edge of a town. I do not like that Africa."

Carla relaxed. "Yes. But we cannot stop the world, can we? Africa has these problems now. We have to try to cope with them."

There was a silence. This woman has not come to talk politics, thought Carla; or African history. Why is she here?

Mma Ramotswe looked at her hands, and at the engagement ring, with its tiny point of light. 'Ten years ago," she began, "you lived out near Molepolole, at that place run by

Burkhardt Fischer. You were there when an American called Michael Curtin disappeared in mysterious circumstances."

She stopped. Carla was staring at her, glassy-eyed.

"I am nothing to do with the police," said Mma Ramotswe, hurriedly. "I have not come here to question you."

Carla's expression was impassive. "Then why do you want to talk about that? It happened a long time ago. He went missing. That's all there is to it."

"No," said Mma Ramotswe. "That is not all there is to it. I don't have to ask you what happened, because I know exactly what took place. You and Oswald Ranta were there, in that hut, when Michael turned up. He fell into a *donga* and broke his neck. You hid the body because Oswald was frightened that the police would accuse him of killing Michael. That is what happened."

Carla said nothing, but Mma Ramotswe saw that her words had shocked her. Dr Ranta had told the truth, as she had thought, and now Carla's reaction was confirming this.

"You did not kill Michael," she said. "It had nothing to do with you. But you did conceal the body, which meant that his mother never found out what happened to him. That was the wrong thing to do. But that's not the point. The point is that you can do something to cancel all that out. You can do that thing quite safely. There is no risk to you."

Carla's voice was distant, barely audible. "What can I do? We can't bring him back."

"You can bring an end to his mother's search," she said. "All she wants to do is to say goodbye to her son. People who have lost somebody are often like that. There may be no desire for revenge in their hearts; they just want to know. That's all."

Carla leaned back in her chair, her eyes downcast. "I don't know ... Oswald would be furious if I talked about ..."

Mma Ramotswe cut her short. "Oswald knows, and

agrees."

"Then why can't he tell her?" retorted Carla, suddenly angry. "He did it. I only lied to protect him."

Mma Ramotswe nodded her understanding. "Yes," she said. "It's his fault, but he is not a good man. He cannot give anything to that woman, or to anybody else for that matter. Such people cannot say sorry to another. But you can. You can meet this woman and tell her what happened. You can seek her forgiveness."

Carla shook her head. "I don't see why ... After all these years ..."

Mma Ramotswe stopped her. "Besides," she said. "You are the mother of her grandchild. Is that not so. Would you deny her that little bit of comfort. She has no son now. But there is a ..."

"Boy," said Carla. "He is called Michael too. He is nine, almost ten."

Mma Ramotswe smiled. "You must bring the child to her, Mma," she said. 'You are a mother. You know what that means. You have no reason now not to do this. Oswald cannot do anything to you. He is no threat."

Mma Ramotswe rose to her feet and walked over to the desk, where Carla sat, crumpled, uncertain.

"You know that you must do this," she said.

She took the other woman's hand and held it gently. It was sun-specked, from exposure to high places and heat, and hard work.

"You will do it, won't you, Mma? She is ready to come out to Botswana. She will come in a day or two if I tell her. Can you get away from here? Just for a few days?"

"I have an assistant," said Carla. 'She can run the place."

"And the boy? Michael? Will he not be happy to see his grandmother?"

Carla looked up at her.

"Yes, Mma Ramotswe," she said. "You are right."

She returned to Gaborone the following day, arriving late at night. Her maid, Rose, had stayed in the house to look after the children, who were fast asleep when Mma Ramotswe arrived home. She crept into their rooms and listened to their soft breathing and smelled the sweet smell of children sleeping. Then exhausted from the drive, she tumbled into her bed, mentally still driving, her eyes moving behind heavy, closed lids.

She was in the office early the following morning, leaving the children in Rose's care. Mma Makutsi had arrived even earlier than she had, and was sitting efficiently behind her desk, typing a report.

"Mr Letsenyane Badule," she announced. "I am reporting on the end of the case."

Mma Ramotswe raised an eyebrow. "I thought that you wanted me to sort that out."

Mma Makutsi pursed her lips. "To begin with, I was not brave enough," she said. "But then he came in yesterday and I had to speak to him. If I had seen him coming, I could have locked the door and put up a closed sign. But he came in before I could do anything about it."

"And?" prompted Mma Ramotswe.

"And I told him about his wife's being unfaithful."

"What did he say?"

"He was upset. He looked very sad."

Mma Ramotswe smiled wryly. "No surprise there," she said.

"Yes, but then I told him that he should not do anything about this as his wife was not doing it for herself, but was doing it for her son's sake. She had taken up with a rich man purely to make sure that his son would get a good education. I said that she was being very selfless. I said that it might be

[199]

best to leave things exactly as they are."

Mma Ramotswe looked astounded. "He believed that?" she said, incredulously.

"Yes," said Mma Makutsi. "He is not a very sophisticated man. He seemed quite pleased."

"I'm astonished," said Mma Ramotswe.

"Well, there you are," said Mma Makutsi. "He remains happy. The wife also continues to be happy. The boy gets his education. And the wife's lover and the wife's lover's wife are also happy. It is a good result."

Mma Ramotswe was not convinced. There was major ethical flaw in this solution, but to define it exactly would require a great deal more thought and discussion. She would have to talk to Mma Makutsi about this at greater length, once she had more time to do so. It was a pity, she thought, that the *Journal of Criminology* did not have a problem page for just such cases. She could have written and asked for advice in this delicate matter. Perhaps she could write to the editor anyway and suggest that an agony aunt be appointed; it would certainly make the journal very much more readable.

Several quiet days ensued, in which, once again, they were without clients, and could bring the administrative affairs of the agency up to date. Mma Makutsi oiled her typewriter and went out to buy a new kettle, for the preparation of bush tea. Mma Ramotswe wrote letters to old friends and prepared accounts for the impending end of the financial year. She had not made a lot of money, but she had not made a loss, and she had been happy and entertained. That counted for infinitely more than a vigorously healthy balance sheet. In fact, she thought, annual accounts should include an item specifically headed *Happiness*, alongside expenses and receipts and the like. That figure in her accounts would be a very large one, she thought.

But it would be nothing to the happiness of Andrea Curtin, who arrived three days later and who met, late that afternoon, in the office of the No. 1 Ladies' Detective Agency, the mother of her grandson and her grandson himself. While Carla was left alone to give the account of what happened on that night ten years ago, Mma Ramotswe took the boy for a walk, and pointed out to him the granite slopes of Kgale Hill and the distant smudge of blue which was the waters of the dam. He was a courteous boy, rather grave in his manner, who was interested in stones, and kept stopping to scratch at some piece of rock or to pick up a pebble.

"This one is quartz," he said, showing her a piece of white rock. "Sometimes you find gold in quartz."

She took the rock and examined it. "You are very interested in rocks?"

"I want to be a geologist," he said solemnly. "We have a geologist who stays in our hotel sometimes. He teaches me about rocks."

She smiled encouragingly. "It would be an interesting job, that," she said. "Rather like being a detective. Looking for things."

She handed the piece of quartz back to him. As he took it, his eye caught her engagement ring, and for a moment he held her hand, looking at the gold band and its twinkling stone.

"Cubic zirconium," he said. "They make them look like diamonds. Just like the real thing."

When they returned, Carla and the American woman were sitting side by side and there was a peacefulness, even joy, in the older woman's expression which told Mma Ramotswe that what she had intended had indeed been achieved.

They drank tea together, just looking at one another. The boy had a gift for his grandmother, a small soapstone carving, which he had made himself. She took it, and kissed him, as any grandmother would.

Mma Ramotswe had a gift for the American woman, a basket which on her return journey from Bulawayo she had bought, on impulse, from a woman sitting by the side of the road in Francistown. The woman was desperate, and Mma Ramotswe, who did not need a basket, had bought it to help her. It was a traditional Botswana basket, with a design worked into the weaving.

"These little marks here are tears," she said. "The giraffe gives its tears to the women and they weave them into the basket."

The American woman took the basket politely, in the proper Botswana way of receiving a gift – with both hands. How rude were people who took a gift with one hand, as if snatching it from the donor; she knew better.

"You are very kind, Mma," she said. "But why did the giraffe give its tears?"

Mma Ramotse shrugged; she had never thought about it. "I suppose that it means that we can all give something," she said. "A giraffe has nothing else to give – only tears." Did it mean that? she wondered. And for a moment she imagined that she saw a giraffe peering down through the trees, its strange, stilt-borne body camouflaged among the leaves; and its moist velvet cheeks and liquid eyes; and she thought of all the beauty that there was in Africa, and of the laughter, and the love.

The boy looked at the basket. "Is that true, Mma?"

Mma Ramotswe smiled.

"I hope so," she said.